WILD YEARS IN WEST BERLIN

Matthias Drawe

Copyright © 2014 Matthias Drawe
All rights reserved.

D.A. Publishing
228 Park Ave S #24579
New York, NY10003
phone: +1-212-486-8049
www.da-publishing.com
info@da-publishing.com

Editor: René Alfaro
Illustrations: Micha Strahl
Berlin in the 1980s: Charles M. Miller
Prologue: Edgar Henry Bukowski

Title also available in German, Spanish, French, and Portuguese.

ISBN: 1508409579
ISBN-13: 978-1508409571

CONTENTS

Prologue

1	Judgment Day	7
2	Community Meeting	11
3	Breakfast	17
4	The Piano	21
5	Jogging	27
6	Street Market	30
7	The Circular Saw	35
8	Heiner's Step Forward	41
9	The Warning	44
10	Safety First	47
11	Colorful Beads	52
12	The Decision	57
13	A Cat Named Fritz	61
14	The Eviction of Blumenthalstrasse	66
15	The Riot	69
16	Wine from the Bottle	75
17	Cough Drops Won't Help	78
18	The Invasion of the Killer Bubbles	83

19	The Search	87
20	The Disease	90
21	The Dream	96
22	The Ultimatum	99
23	The Concert	101
24	Smog	114
25	Heiner's Offer	118
26	The Power Drill	121
27	The Water Connection	125
28	Kalle and Socke	128
29	The Shopping Committee	131
30	The Anniversary Celebration	136
31	The Abyss	146
32	As Luck Would Have It	148
	About the Author	153
	Berlin in the 1980s	154

PROLOGUE

We are in a squatted house in West Berlin in the early 80s. Every day is a battle against the elements. Sometimes it's the cops looking for drugs, sometimes a bunch of skinheads smashing windows, or it's Frau Steinmöller again, the lovely neighbor from across the street.

Fortunately, the squatters always manage to outsmart their enemies. Only "special needs" Heiner is a tough nut to crack since he just won't let go.

Adding to the supreme madness is the fact that the trials and tribulations of our brave, anarchist squatters happen on a "capitalist island" - surrounded by a booby-trapped wall and an absurd communist regime.

1.
JUDGMENT DAY

After Heiner's plunge, it was all over. Two days after the ambulance had picked him up, the cops moved in. Ten combat units. At five o'clock in the morning.

When the battering ram blew the front door off its hinges, the entire house shook. Hucky knew what was coming. He heard boots pounding up the stairs and distorted yelling through a megaphone. Seconds later, the door flew open: Three cops in combat uniforms. They probably thought he would resist, forming a triangle in front of his bed but he just said: "Easy, guys, I'm coming."

Hucky dressed deliberately slow. He heard Lilli scream next door. Her body hit the wall and glass shattered. Lilli was skinny, but when she was angry, she could develop unbelievable strength. The cops dragged her into the hallway. She screamed, wriggled back and forth, biting around. But finally they subdued her and carried her along the corridor. Her pink T-shirt had ridden up over her private parts.

A police line separated the squatters from the house. Everybody in the street seemed to be awake, and people stared out of their windows. It was cold.

"Great!" shouted the old hag from across the street. "Finally, this riff-raff will be locked up."
Gerlinde Steinmöller always gawked out her window on the fourth floor and meddled in just everything.
"Screw yourself, sweetie," shouted Candy and showed her the finger.

Lilli sobbed, and Falk gave her a hug. Kermit, Candy, and Pflaume stood motionless and kept a straight face. Kugelblitz spat beside him on the floor.

This time the cops had brought bricklayers. After the windows were bricked up, the head honcho let the squatters in again to get their things. Separately. And just three minutes each.

Hucky grabbed his guitar and the amp. He took one last look into his room: His red curtains with the squatter logo, the sleeping platform, which he had built from scrap wood and his old tube radio.

His eyes fell on the Sex Pistols poster on the door. Damn, the poster was worth more than anything. Some years ago he had hitchhiked with only 20 marks in his pocket to Amsterdam to see one of the first Pistols concerts. At the time almost nobody had heard of them in Germany. And he had even managed to get Steve Jones's autograph.

He carefully loosened the poster from the door, rolled it up, and stuck it into his t-shirt.

He cast a last look into the kitchen and into their community room, remembering how they had fixed up the house together. He thought of the improvised roof garden, their lunches on the patio, and the fresh eggs from the chicken coop. But now, it seemed, all of this had come to an end. And why? - It was damn Heiner's fault. It had all started when he showed up at their community meeting half a year ago.

2.
COMMUNITY MEETING

The meeting was set for Mondays at eight, which basically meant it started around nine. At twenty to nine Hucky peered through the door of the community room. Not a soul. He went into the kitchen, but it was empty as well.

He strolled back to the community room, sat down on a mattress and rolled a smoke. Somebody had to be the first, obviously. Almost the entire room was covered with old mattresses, and in the center stood a flat table with a heart-shaped ashtray. The windows were patched in places with transparent plastic foil, and the stove pipe ran through the entire room. It was more heat efficient this way.

Hucky blew smoke in the air and looked at his feet. He had bought a pair of Doc Martens, secondhand. They were a bit worn already, but it was even better this way. His jeans were greasy and torn in some places, and his homemade T-shirt read: "NeVEr mINd thE bOLLOCkS."

Pflaume and Candy came in. They settled down on a mattress and leaned their backs against the wall. "Let me roll one, buddy."

Pflaume had thick lips and an overbite. His black Mohawk spiked more than eight inches high, and it stood like a rock. Occasionally his heavy Swabian accent came through.

Candy was skinny and had bad teeth. Her pink colored hair spilled out from under her black leather cap, and her black net-shirt revealed an impressive cleavage.

Eventually the others showed up: Falk, Lilli, Kermit, Carla, and Kugelblitz. Meike sat next to Hucky. She was a bit chubby, had brown button eyes and her short black hair stood in all directions. She wore a dog collar with chrome spikes.

Falk leaned his back against the wall and flicked his long hair from his forehead. He had acne scars on the cheeks, and on one side he was missing a molar. Falk, Pflaume, and Candy had started the squat almost three years ago. All others had joined later.
"Quiet, please," Falk said. "Calm down, folks! Can we begin now?"

At this moment, Heiner squeezed through the door.

Hucky had never seen the guy before. He sat down on the mattress next to Kermit, and Hucky thought that the two might have known each other from olden days in East Germany.

It was obvious that something was not quite right with Heiner. His style did absolutely not fit in. He wore a white bobble hat with a pom-pom, a Norwegian reindeer sweater, brown corduroy pants, and sandals that showed natural wool socks. He also sported a neatly trimmed full beard.

Falk took a piece of paper out of his pocket and read the different items on the agenda: The faulty fuses in the basement, the worn lock on the front door, and the water supply. The water supply was a real problem. When the house had stood vacant, the connection had been cut, which meant that they had to use canisters to bring in water.

Falk read a letter from the city council. The house would get a new water connection if they would sign a contract. Pflaume yawned and said, "Blah, blah, blah ..." Kugelblitz shouted, "Screw them." And Candy said, "I'd rather carry a thousand canisters before talking to those bastards."

And that was that.

They talked about the fuses that constantly blew and could not be repaired with aluminum foil anymore. Kermit said that he would take care of this. He knew of an abandoned public gym nearby where he could unscrew a few fuses.

Hucky glanced at Lilli. She looked damn good, even with the weird Inca beanie that she wore lately. She sat by the window, staring into the night. The meeting did not interest her in the least, and she kept on scribbling something on a piece of paper. Hucky suspected that it was full moon again. At full moon, she always acted strangely.

Lilli stood up and vanished. She had left the paper with the scribble on the mattress: A ruffled crow was sitting on a power line. Below the drawing it read *Kredenka mutakrak!* Hucky pulled the piece of paper casually towards him and pocketed it.

Suddenly Heiner spoke up. He scrambled to his feet, so everybody could see him. He wanted to move in.

It was quiet at once, and everybody gawked at the strange fellow. "Huh?" Candy said. "This guy wants to move in? Anybody knows him?"
"I am in favor, folks," Kugelblitz shouted. "New people are always good. I am in favor!"
"Quiet, guys." Falk flicked his hair from his forehead. "Let him have a word."

Heiner was a bit weak on his feet and sat down again. A cat jumped on his lap and he stroked it. "Well, actually, I wanted to ask if you would have use for a piano and a circular saw. I would have to store them somewhere."
"A piano?" said Carla. "Yeah, man!"
"Bring it on," Kugelblitz shouted. "We sure can use it."
"A piano ...?" Falk scratched his head. "Actually not a bad idea ..."

Hucky definitely did not want the piano. He was pretty sure that they would use it with T.T. Embargo once it stood there. In Hucky's view T.T. Embargo was a classic guitar band, not a freaking orchestra. Falk's flute solos were already hardly bearable, and a piano was simply too much. However, a circular saw would certainly come handy. Hundreds of old railway ties were strewn on the S-Bahn premises, and with the saw they could cut them up and save on heating costs.

"Why us?" Meike asked. "We do not even know you."
"Exactly," Candy said. "There are plenty of other squats around."
Heiner stroked the cat. "Well, I've looked at the building closely and it would simply be perfect for the type of program I have in mind. And it would also be pretty easy to install an elevator."
"An elevator ...?" Falk raised his eyebrows.
"What do you mean, an elevator?" Kermit said. "Are you insane, man?"
"You've probably noticed that I am a person with special needs, right?" He pointed to his skinny legs.
"Yeah, so what?" said Kermit.
"Well, you wouldn't want to carry me up the stairs each time, would you?"

Heiner was a spastic. When walking he wobbled back and forth, waving his arms. It took him half an hour to climb two flights of stairs.

"It probably wouldn't be such a big deal to carry you up," Falk said. "But we hardly know you, man, I mean, actually we don't know you at all."
"Exactly," Meike said. "If somebody knew you ..."
"Sure, that's obvious," Heiner said. "But that's exactly why I'm here."

The meeting lasted two hours already. Pflaume felt his belly and looked at Candy. He was hungry and wanted to grab a kebab. He tapped his wrist. "What's the freakin' time?"
"Gotta go as well," Kugelblitz said and stood up. "Shall we?"
Pflaume put on his jacket and checked whether his Mohawk stood up neatly.

Falk looked at Heiner. "Maybe you'll just stop by couple of times for breakfast, or so, around eleven or twelve, or is there anything urgent with you?"
The cat jumped from Heiner's lap and ran out the door.
"For me, nothing's urgent," he said. "But I need to get the piano out of the moist basement. That would be the most pressing thing right now."
"Sure, sure," Falk said. "No problem, pal. We'll put it in the store downstairs."

Pflaume grabbed Candy's hand and pulled her up. He tapped two fingers against his temple: "See ya!"
Suddenly, the others stood up as well and the community room emptied.

Heiner scrambled to his feet and rowed out the door.

3.

BREAKFAST

Hucky stood in the kitchen doing the dishes, Kugelblitz boiled water for coffee, and Meike wiped the table clean.

Following the meeting Meike had come to Hucky's room, and after a few beers and some shots of vodka, it had, of course, happened again.

Hucky had slept with Meike several times already, but unfortunately it was not what he really wanted. That's why he kept her at bay in public. She had tried to kiss him in front of the others several times, but he had made it clear in a loving way, that this was not his thing. End of story. Or so he thought.

Hucky tipped the water container over the edge of the sink and washed the dishes. The drain pipe was cut off in the middle, and the dirt water ran into a bucket which they later used to flush the toilet.

Lilli had painted the fridge black. Around the kitchen table stood a wooden bench, a few stools and two empty beer crates. The lamp shade was made from the drum of a washing machine.

Suddenly the door burst open: Pflaume. Naked. His Mohawk lay flat and covered one ear. Pflaume scratched his butt, yawned, and disappeared again. Before he got up, he always checked whether something was going on already.

Carla brought the eggs from the chicken coop. "Morning everyone!" She wore a blue uniform jacket with gold buttons. If it was not too cold, she walked barefoot.

Three months ago they had bought ten chickens. They were roaming freely on the patio in the back yard. Their cackling could be heard in the kitchen. Carla took three eggs and juggled them. Suddenly she threw an egg past behind her back and caught it in front. Carla was good. Hucky had seen her juggle several times, and she had never broken an egg.

Slowly the others trickled in. Falk stretched and yawned. "*Buenos días*, everyone." He liked to throw in a bit of Spanish once in a while. He thought it was cool. His hair was greasy and stood out in all directions. As always in the morning he was wearing only an unbuttoned shirt and baggy underpants. Shortly after, Lilli walked in. She wore the Inca beanie again and whistled "Somewhere over the rainbow." Probably Falk had just banged her again. The two mated like rabbits.

Lilli sipped coffee, sat down cross-legged on the bench and began to crochet a tiny shoe. Was she making baby clothes?

Although spring had officially started, it had become colder again. There was a large hole under the flue where the old coal oven had stood. A sign on the wall read: "Kerm's fireplace." Kermit wanted to build an open fireplace there, but he claimed that he had not yet all the materials together. He chewed on a bread roll and said, "I'll start tomorrow, for real!"

Kermit looked a bit like the famous frog. He never combed his curly hair, and it had morphed into dreadlocks. In his room he had a huge, homemade bong, which could be dismantled in seven and a half seconds.

Kermit hailed from East Germany and had belonged to a skateboard clique there. Of course you could not buy skateboards in the East and therefore they had just built them at home. That alone was enough to be considered subversive. Eventually he had ended up in jail, and the West had bought him out.

Hucky smeared a bread roll with strawberry jam and sipped some hot coffee. Meike sat opposite him and gave him the look.

Suddenly she threw him an air kiss.

Hucky acted as if he had not noticed it and looked out the window. It was a delicate matter. Especially because he owed her 250 marks.

Meike worked in a health food store and was the only one in the house who earned money regularly. All others lived on welfare or did odd jobs here and there. Pflaume received a parcel with Swabian delicacies from his mother every two weeks, and Kugelblitz tapped into his grandma occasionally.

After breakfast they smoked and played "Anarchy in the UK" on the tape recorder. The kitchen window looked out onto the S-Bahn premises. The line was no longer operational due to the division of the city. Twice a day an empty train rode along the line so that the tracks would not get rusty.

"Quiet," Kermit said. "I think, someone rang the bell."

Pflaume turned down the music. There was only one bell for the entire house, and it was on the ground floor. Sometimes it was hard to hear. It rang again.
"Who can it be, at this time?" said Kermit. "The cops don't ring the bell, do they?"

4.
THE PIANO

It was Heiner. He had come to get help moving the piano and had brought carrying straps. Of course, no one wanted to pick it up.

Pflaume said: "Need to stop by at Welfare," and Candy said: "No way."

Hucky quickly snuck away as well. If Falk wanted the piano, let him carry it. He peered out his window and saw Falk, Carla, and Heiner get into their old Ford Transit. The battered van was registered in Falk's name, but they shared the insurance.

Hucky grabbed his guitar and played the first few riffs of "God Save the Queen, the fascist regime." Simply brilliant. Why on earth had he not come up with something like that? Steve Jones was a genius. He had created a unique style without even knowing how to read music. Or maybe just because of that.

Hucky had bought himself a used Gibson Les Paul. Just the model Steve Jones played. Or rather, it was a Gibson replica from Ibanez. But it looked like the Gibson, and the sound was virtually identical. Cleverly, he had pasted the anarchist "circle A" over the Ibanez logo.

He played a song that he had composed for T.T. Embargo: "Living in a squat, dududu-duuh, dududu-duuh..., sometimes cold, sometimes hot, dududu-duuh, dududu-duuh ..."

Steve Jones played through a Marshall, now, but Hucky could not afford one. The only option had been an old, beat-up Fender Reverb from the flea market. But Steve Jones had played through a Fender Reverb as well in the beginning. Hucky had seen it in Amsterdam with his very eyes.

Hucky hailed from the quaint West German town of Bad Wildungen and his real name was Holger von Hachenstein. But this needed to remain a secret. Both, Bad Wildungen and the "von" were simply bullshit.
If Hucky stood in front of the mirror and said "Hucky," it simply fit. "Holger von Hachenstein" did not. Ironically, the "von" was even totally worthless. Impoverished gentry. No property, no land, no connections.

Hucky played the first verse of his song again: "Living in a squat, dududu-duuh, dududu-duuh..., sometimes cold, sometimes hot, dududu-duuh, dududu-duuh ..."

Suddenly Lilli stood in the doorway. She held a pink crochet outfit in hand: a tiny Inca beanie, a matching tiny sweater and two tiny shoes.
"How do you like it?" she asked.

Hucky did not know what to say. Were those baby clothes?

"Want to apply for the art academy", Lilly said. "Need to submit something. Have a cigarette?"

Lilli sat down beside him on his platform bed and rolled one. She resembled Amanda Lear. Even her stupid Inca beanie could not hide it. Hucky glanced at her from the side. Her body was lean as always, so maybe she wasn't pregnant, and the crochet clothes were really for the academy.

As a teenager, Hucky had purchased the hit single "Follow Me" in the only record store of Bad Wildungen. Of course he had done so mainly because of Amanda Lear's topless picture on the cover. Admittedly Hucky had not understood the entire text of the song, but it had been enough. "Follow Me" was exactly what he wanted.

The purchase of the single had practically been an illegal act. Hucky had waited until no one was in the store. His father, Helmuth von Hachenstein, senior teacher of Latin and math at the local high school, could never know how Hucky spent his pocket money. Lithe as a thief, he had slipped into the store and quickly pulled "Follow Me" from the shelf. Of course, he knew exactly where it was. The vendor grinned, since Hucky had not been the first teenager who bought the record, blushing.

Lilli smoked. Her eyes darted nervously back and forth. Hucky suddenly heard the tune of "Follow Me" in his mind's ear: "I'm moving out …, I'm getting on …, and from now on …, address unknown …"
He felt a tingle in his stomach. Lilli had been in his room before to bum cigarettes, but she had never sat down. She glanced at the Pistols poster on the door, but did not comment on it. Lilli went for Led Zeppelin. She constantly listened to "Stairway to Heaven." Especially at full moon.

Actually, Hucky was not a big fan of the song. He found it a bit lame, but to impress Lilli one day, he had listened to the record over and over and had painstakingly heard out the intro. The right moment had finally come. He grabbed his guitar and played "Stairway to Heaven."

Lilli raised her eyebrows, impressed.

Then came the best part, Hucky let his fingers elegantly slide over the fretboard: "Duh-dee, duh-dummmm ..."

Somebody honked. Lilli rushed to the window. "Falk!"

The Transit with the piano had arrived, and Lilli ran downstairs. Hucky put the guitar aside, frustrated. Poor timing again. When Lilli had joined the squat, he had been too hesitant. Falk had immediately hit on her and managed to bang her on the second day.

The piano was a gem. Glossy black finish. Heiner had inherited it from his grandma. As it stood on the sidewalk, they all hammered on the keys.

Gerlinde Steinmöller peeked out her window. "Stop that noise, you idiots!" she shouted. "Shut up, dammit!"

Carla showed her the *Peace* sign, sat on a crate and played the beginning of "Imagine." Hucky was stunned. He had no idea that Carla could play the piano. She started to sing: "Imagine there's no heaven ... it's easy if you try ..., no hell below us ... above us only sky ..."
Suddenly she had forgotten the lyrics and hit the wrong keys.

It started to drizzle. They tried to hoist the piano into the store but it was damn heavy and bulky. It had impossible measurements.
Heiner stood inside and gave orders. He was afraid that a scratch could come to the piano. "Stop, stop," he shouted. "This way we'll never get it in. You have to start out exactly straight."

The door was not wide enough. Or rather, the piano might just have fit through, but it was a precision job. They tried it three times. Then Kugelblitz slumped against the wall and groaned. Pflaume looked at the welts in his hands. "Sorry, guys, but I am not going to kill myself."

Hucky was also exhausted and felt an unpleasant sting in his lower back.
But then Carla had a brilliant idea. They walked over to the

Karadeniz, a Turkish tea house across the street. That's where they always filled their water canisters. The Turks were really cool and asked no stupid questions.

There were only men in the Karadeniz. They smoked and played cards. A teapot sat on a hot plate, and on the wall behind the counter hung a picture of Atatürk. Ismail, the owner, was half bald and had a bushy black mustache with gray streaks. He crossed the street with them, measured the door, the piano, then the door again. He shook his head.

"This no going work like this, friends."

The Turks brought a few tools from the Karadeniz and lifted the door off its hinges. Then they placed a ramp on the threshold and put the piano on a wheeled platform. Finally, they pushed the massive instrument gently into the house.
The crowd cheered. Heiner shook Ismail's hand and said: "Really don't know how to thank you, guys, you were fantastic!"
"No problem, my friend," Ismail said. He lit a cigarette, and the Turks went back into their tea house.

Heiner's piano stood safe and sound in the store, now. So did his circular saw and an old bed frame that he had brought as well.
Hucky suddenly felt back pain: first, because the piano had been so damn heavy, and second, because he was totally out of shape. He desperately needed to do something for his body.

5.

JOGGING

Hucky trotted up the slope next to the S-Bahn premises. Easy! The elastic band of his sweatpants was worn out, and he had strapped a belt around his waist.

A beautiful day. Flocks of birds passed over the abandoned S-Bahn premises, landed in trees and flew up again. Just a few minutes into trotting up the slope, Hucky began to sweat, his legs were getting heavier. He stared at the large steel bridge leading over the S-Bahn tracks. He wanted to hold out at least until he reached the bridge.

Suddenly he felt a sharp sting in his side and had to stop. Something was wrong with his rhythm. He leaned against a billboard and panted, feeling sharp stings in his side. Probably the cigarettes were to blame. And too much beer and cheap vodka. And occasionally Kermit's bong. Anyway, he needed to force himself to go on. He really was a wimp, if he gave up this fast.

Hucky trotted on and pressed both hands against his rib cage. Eventually, the stings ceased. He ran across the old steel bridge and along the cemetery wall. His t-shirt was soaked with sweat.

He passed the gate of the cemetery and glanced at the headstones. There they lay and rotted in their cold tombs.

He wondered how he would go, once his day had come. Uh, bullshit, after all, he was still young.

He sat down on a bench at the cemetery wall, closed his eyes and relaxed. Somewhere he had read that Steve Jones did absolutely nothing to keep fit. He simply gave it his all on stage and lost almost a gallon of fluid at each gig.

Hucky stood up and stretched his legs. On stage, he had to be lithe as a cat. He tried to reach his left heel behind his back with his right hand. He couldn't. He was too stiff. He tried again with momentum but almost tipped over backwards.

An elderly couple walked past him. The woman carried flowers in her arms, the man a watering can. They disappeared in the cemetery.

He trotted back home. In the far distance he saw the S-Bahn underpass. That was his goal. He panted from one lamp post to the next. Then he saw the back of their house.

Almost there! With his last strength he trotted through the underpass. Just then, Lilli came out the front door. Although it was quite warm, she wore the Inca beanie again. "Hey, Hucky, you're all sweaty!"
He trotted next to her on the spot. No one knew where exactly she came from. Just like Heiner, she had one day appeared at the weekly meeting and, since everybody liked her, moved in the same day.

Supposedly, her mother was Vietnamese and her father a French marine officer, but Hucky doubted it. Once he had seen her chatting with the Yugo from the chicken grill. She spoke fluent Serbo-Croatian, but her mother was Vietnamese and her father French? That made absolutely no sense. He had visited the public library to find out what *Kredenka mutakrak!* meant. It wasn't Serbo-Croatian. Neither Czech nor Polish. And certainly not Vietnamese.

Hucky still trotted next to Lilli on the spot. "*Kredenka mutakrak!*"
She looked at him, puzzled. "Huh?"
She did not understand her own secret language. Probably she had forgotten what she had scrawled under her drawing.
Hucky trotted past her and energetically jumped up the stairs, always three steps at a time. When he was outside her sight, he tipped against the wall, gasping for air.

Now it was certain. Lilli was crazy.

6.
STREET MARKET

Twice a week there was a market along the block. They sold vegetables, fruit, eggs, bread, and knick-knack. Most vendors were Turks. It began quite early and usually woke Hucky up.
The guy who sold bananas always seemed to have a stuffy nose. He shouted with a humming sound: "Come to me, come to me, bananas, nice and big, just two marks. Just two marks the bunch!"

Hucky looked out of the window. A beautiful day. The sky was blue. The Turk from the vegetable stand shouted: "Three kilos for five! Three kilos for five! Yes, young lady, tomatoes, so red, so beautiful, so super tasty!"

At the street corner, next to the chicken grill, stood a phone booth. Sometimes Hucky called his mother from there. He couldn't call her at home, because daddy had imposed a communication ban. This made it a bit more complicated but it worked anyway. He just called his sister, who then asked mom to come over. The last time his mother had been in tears. They had not seen each other for almost two years. Hucky's eyes had also been moist. Luckily no one had seen him. T.T. Embargo's guitarist simply did not cry. And certainly not when speaking with his mom.

Bad Wildungen and West Berlin were two completely different planets. What was the highlight of the year in Bad Wildungen? The Flower Parade in mid-September of course. 400,000 dahlias lovingly arranged on floats. Along the parade they had a beer festival in the old town where the "Flower Queen" was elected. And what else?

Actually, not that much.

Hucky remembered the day he arrived in West Berlin. He saw it in front of him as if it had been yesterday. The guy who had given him a ride through the murky East, had dropped him off early in the morning in Neukölln.
Hucky was dead tired but still had to take the subway to the other end of town. His buddy Carl lived in Wedding. Hailing from Bad Wildungen as well, he had, like Hucky, dodged the draft. The West German army had no authority in West Berlin, where the Four Power Agreement ruled.

The subway rumbled along as Hucky looked at the other passengers. Some seemed to travel to work, others looked like they were coming from the night shift.
Hucky closed his eyes for a moment. The long drive through pitch black East Germany had exhausted him. In addition, there had been a long wait at the checkpoint into West Berlin. The East German border guards had searched every single car.
The subway stopped at Kottbusser Tor, and Hucky woke up. A group of young revelers streamed into the wagon. A cheerful, colorful bunch. And not a bit tired at half after five in the morning.

Shortly after Moritzplatz the train drove into one of the ghost stations, squeaking loudly. At this stretch, the subway travelled under the center of East Berlin. The West had bought the using rights. The train did not stop, but just drove by at reduced speed. East German border guards, armed with machine guns, stood on the platforms. Otherwise, the stations still looked like the time when the Wall had been built, only here and there a few tiles had fallen off. There was even a faded poster, advertising a track and field event in 1961.

Hucky got off at Voltastrasse. Daylight had come up by now, but it was cloudy, and everything was gray, the sky, the cobblestones, the dilapidated buildings that still had bullet holes from World War II. After a couple of yards the street was cut off by the Wall.

On the other side was East Berlin. The bright lights of the death strip were still on. Right next to the wall two Turks repaired an old Ford Consul. Coal briquettes were delivered at one of the buildings.

In Berlin they still burned coal in tile stoves, just like one hundred years ago!

Hucky felt a shiver down his spine, and he knew immediately that he had come to the right place. He could literally smell history, and not just because of the coal dust and the industrial pollution from the East. He saw the Red Army soldiers who had conquered the city in 1945 in murderous street fighting and fleeing Nazi hordes that were trying to save their skin. Even Adolf was somehow still present, since those were exactly the streets, which he had passed with his armored Mercedes. And with a little imagination you could even see Kaiser Wilhelm as he trotted on his white horse over the cobblestones.

"Three kilos for five! Three kilos for five!" The Turk from the vegetable stand gave it his all again: "Yes, young lady, tomatoes, so red, so beautiful, so super tasty!"
Hucky still stood by his window and looked down at the market. Almost two years had passed since his escape to Berlin and he had absolutely no regrets. Quite to the contrary, he had the feeling that he was exactly at the right place at the right time.

Meike and Kermit waited below with two large bags. They had been hiding behind a corner. The city's waste collection made a detour around the house, so they had to get rid of their garbage somewhere else. When the guys of market surveillance were out of sight, Meike and Kermit crept up from behind to the waste containers and threw their trash bags in.

As always Gerlinde Steinmöller sat by her window across

33

the street. She had observed everything with her opera binoculars and picked up the phone. Probably she called market supervision, now. But the bags were in, and Meike and Kermit had already disappeared in the crowd.

The market was a gift from the gods. It not only helped with the garbage disposal, but it even fed the house. At the end of the day the vendors just threw the leftovers away. Much of it was still perfectly okay, and the squatters collected it.

Hucky suddenly saw Heiner come wobbling around the corner. As always, he had this ungainly gait as he flailed his arms. It was strange: From above, it almost seemed as if Meike and Heiner attracted each other magnetically. They steered though the thick crowd of the market and almost collided at an apple stand.

Heiner chatted Meike up and came pretty close to her. Actually, too close. Then he scribbled something on a piece of paper.

Did he want to hit on her?

7.
THE CIRCULAR SAW

Hucky and Kugelblitz had decided to cut the railway ties from the S-Bahn premises with Heiner's table saw. They set it up in the store downstairs. Kugelblitz turned it on, and the blade slowly traveled up. Until now they had cut the ties with a hand saw, which took forever.

They picked up the first tie and put it on the table. They were not quite sure if the saw was up to snuff. The wood was damn hard, and could possibly break the blade.

They pushed the tie warily forward. The blade cut through the wood - almost as if it were butter. In a matter of seconds they had cut the tie in half.
"Not bad," Hucky said. Kugelblitz gave the thumbs up. "Yeah, absolutely amazing, man!"

Kugelblitz was short and had the onset of a beer belly. Despite this, he was surprisingly nimble and fast. Occasionally he twirled the fuzzy beard on his chin.

They threw the cut pieces on a pile and worked their way through the railway ties.

Suddenly Lilli appeared, a tattered book under her arm: *Piano in Four Weeks*. She walked to the piano, which stood in the other corner of the store. She opened her book and

35

practiced a few finger exercises. It did not seem to bother her that Hucky and Kugelblitz made a hell of a noise with the saw. She simply continued with her exercise and turned the pages of her book.

Hucky looked at Lilli's slender neck. He had dreamed about her the previous night – a wild, erotic dream. It did not bother him that she was crazy. Quite the opposite.

Next to the piano stood Pflaume's drum set. That's where he always practiced. - Hucky remembered the fateful afternoon almost two years ago when he had walked past the squat for the very first time and heard a muffled drum beat eminating from ground floor. The building looked completely different from all the others in the street. A flag with the squatter logo flew from a window, and a plastic skeleton with a Mohawk made of bicycle spokes hung on a ledge.

Shortly after his arrival in Berlin Hucky had started to look for a place to stay. The search was more difficult than expected. Even a small room in a shared apartment was hard to get, and he could not stay much longer with his buddy Carl. The place was a small studio on the ground floor in the backyard. The toilet was across the hall and shared with the guy next door. It was dark and damp, and you never saw the sun. That's why Hucky spent almost all his time outdoors taking along his guitar. He practiced in public parks.

As Hucky stood before the squatted house he peered through a crack of the old door. Inside the store sat a guy with a Mohawk rehearsing a drum beat. It was quite dark because all the windows were barricaded. Only a bare bulb directly above the drums gave some light. Suddenly the door opened, squeaking. It had not been locked.

Directly behind Hucky stood the afternoon sun, and his body and the guitar case cast a long shadow into the store.

Pflaume stopped drumming. He squinted against the bright light and looked at the intruder. He pointed with one of his sticks at Hucky's guitar case. "Can you play?"

Hucky nodded.

Pflaume motioned to an old tube radio with an adapter for a guitar cable. Hucky plugged in and played the intro to "Anarchy in the UK." Pflaume grinned. He knew the song of course and fell into the rhythm. They sang together: "I ...

am ... the Antichrist, ... I ... am ... an anarchist ..."

The tube radio didn't have much amp power, but it worked somehow. Actually it distorted quite beautifully. Hucky and Pflaume roared "... 'cause Iiiiiiii, wanna beeeeeee, ... anarchyyyyyy!" But then Pflaume missed a beat, and they both fell out of rhythm.

"Dammit, I slipped," Pflaume cursed.

Hucky played the intro to "Message in a Bottle." It had taken him days to figure out the guitar track by listening to the record over and over. But now he had it down, and it was pure bliss. Pflaume raised his eyebrows in awe. The beat of "Message in a Bottle" was infinitely more difficult than "Anarchy in the UK." He tapped on the cymbal and beat in syncopation on the snare drum. He certainly was no Stewart Copeland, but he could at least keep the beat.
Hucky played the bridge to the chorus and suddenly, out of nowhere, crystal clear vocals set in. "... I'll send an SOS to the world ... I'll send an SOS to the world ..."

It was magical, where the hell did the vocals come from? Falk jumped out of the darkness on an upturned crate. Unnoticed he had turned on his vocal amp and plugged in a microphone. Then came the transition to the climax of the song. Falk closed his eyes and pressed it out. "I hope that someone gets my, I hope that someone gets my ... message in a boooottle..." Pflaume beat like a madman on the drums, and Hucky got goose bumps. Their chemistry was unbelievable. - Just two days later, he had moved in.

"Buzzzz!" Kugelblitz and Hucky cut another railroad tie. They were almost halfway through the pile when Heiner showed up at the store. He had a half-eaten apple in his mouth and measured the room with a tape measure.

Kugelblitz raised his eyebrows. "What the hell is he doing?" Heiner stood behind Lilli and watched her playing the piano. Once he even tapped his finger on a key and grinned at her.

Suddenly the saw stopped. In the middle of a tie it simply gave up. Kugelblitz switched the power button off, on, off, on, but the saw didn't work anymore.

Heiner had noticed that something was wrong. "Any problem?"

"It's dead," Kugelblitz said. Heiner frowned. He looked at the saw from under the table, pondered a moment and pressed the power button. Nothing.

"I don't get it," Kugelblitz said. "We've merely cut a few pieces of wood ..."

"Sure," Heiner said. "But you probably didn't do it right."

"What do you mean, didn't do it right? Sawing is sawing."

"Not, necessarily. It really wouldn't be so bad, guys, if the saw belonged to me at least."

"It's not yours?" Hucky asked.

"No. I only keep it for somebody."

Heiner crawled under the table and fiddled with the saw. He slapped his hand against his forehead and suddenly knew what it was. The saw had become too hot, and the fuse had automatically turned it off. They waited a while, and the saw was working again. "Well," Heiner said, grinning. "Know-how is king, see? Just be a bit careful from now on, okay?" He took up the tape measure again and nibbled his apple. "Need to talk to Falk."

He went up the stairs and painstakingly pulled himself up at the hand rail.

Suddenly it dawned on Hucky why Heiner had measured everything: It was because of the elevator. If he wanted to build one, he needed the exact measurements.

8.
HEINER'S STEP FORWARD

Heiner had figured out that Meike didn't eat meat, and had invited her to a vegetarian restaurant. He had a couple of coupons for it and knew one of the owners.

Hucky and Meike were alone in the kitchen. She stood at the stove and cooked something for community dinner. The veggies were the remains from the market, and Meike had received some complimentary rice from the health food store. In addition, she often brought expired bread which still tasted perfectly fine, especially if you toasted it.

Hucky was sitting at the table and drank a glass of red wine. Even the wine was free. Candy's sister worked in a supermarket in Marienfelde. There, they had dusted off a whole batch of French country wine, because the bottles had been delivered with faulty labels. They had picked up the fifty boxes with the van, and subsequently had turned into wine drinkers.

Meike talked about the vegetarian dinner with Heiner. They had been sitting at a table for two by candlelight. Heiner had looked deep into her eyes and had said things like: "The sesame sauce is really delicious, is it not?"
"Well, he does have beautiful eyes," Meike said. "And if you only look at his upper part … Have you ever noticed his eyes?"

41

"Not really," Hucky said. "It would be interesting to know, how the hanky-panky works with him. Do you think it works at all?"

"Dumbass," Meike said.

Sure, admittedly it was a stupid question, but somehow it was the point, and Hucky suddenly understood why Heiner wanted to move in. He probably thought that he could easily get laid in the squat. But he had it terribly wrong.

It was not easier than anywhere else.

Sure, on the whole, it was a bit more relaxed. There were no doors in the bathrooms, and almost always somebody walked by when you sat on the throne, or someone simply ran down the corridor naked, but this was just part of the general vibe. If you could not pee when somebody stood next to you, you were an uptight bourgeois. But the real thing, the sex itself, was as private as anywhere.

In any case, Heiner was a strange fellow, and Hucky suspected that he had never had a woman.

When they sat together at dinner, they found out that Heiner had tried to "help" everybody in the squat at least once. Actually, he merely wanted to be good, but it totally backfired.

"I was dismantling a few floorboards on the second floor," Kermit said, "when he suddenly stood behind me and wanted to know what I'm doing. The floor would be totally okay, still, and there would be no need to rip out the floorboards. He didn't know of course that the support beams below are totally rotten anyway ..."

"For two hours he explained the plans to his elevator to

me," Falk said. "At the end I thought, I'm a wire rope myself."

"I just don't feel him, man," Candy said. "It's as simple as that."

Meike defended Heiner. She thought he just didn't get the vibe, yet.
"He's just a plain asshole," Pflaume said. "He will never get it. If it were for me, screw the piano and the saw."
"Give him a chance," Meike said. "I sincerely feel he's not a bad person, only a bit weird."

Candy shoveled some veggie risotto in her mouth. "This guy will never change, girl," she said chewing. "I know this type. He's a damn wiseass."

9.
THE WARNING

Hucky was still in bed when the door burst open and Kermit stormed in.

"The cops are downstairs," he screamed, "The cops, five units!" Kermit ran on to Lilli's room and screamed again: "The cops, the cops."

Hucky jumped up and ran down to the third floor balcony. Behind him were Lilli in her pink t-shirt and Falk in underpants and worn-out sneakers. What the hell did the cops want now? It was the third time this month that they showed up in front of the house.

The squatters stood on the balcony and looked down. Five combat vans were parked on the other side of the street. The cops still sat inside. Through the barred windows, one could see that they were wearing helmets. A crowd had gathered at the corner with the chicken grill. The Turks from the Karadeniz stood on the street, and Gerlinde Steinmöller observed everything with her opera binoculars.

It was quiet. Suddenly, two cops stepped out. The first wore only a cap. He was obviously in charge. The other one dropped his helmet and tucked it under the arm. The two talked, looked up and down the street. They did not even take notice of the squatters.

Falk, Hucky, and Kermit put a couple of bricks on the balustrade. Pflaume and Kugelblitz secured the front door on the ground floor with a railway tie. Some more cops stepped out of their vehicles and consulted with the first two.

It was windy. Candy had her lips pressed tightly together. Suddenly she could no longer control herself and screamed:

"Assholes!"

The cops looked up. One pulled out a walkie-talkie and spoke into it. Three went to the cargo doors of the vehicles and said something to the cops sitting inside.

They were ready to strike.

Falk's hands were clenched around the balustrade. Lilli grabbed a brick and held it ostentatiously in the air. The guy with the walkie-talkie suddenly got radio contact and reported to the chief.

The chief looked at his watch, pondered, pulled up the zipper of his jacket and waved everyone to get back into the vehicles. A few seconds later they were gone.

Lilli put the brick back on the floor and sighed. "I really thought this was it."
"Nah," said Falk. "They were just bluffing."
Candy kicked the balcony door open. "If somebody needs me, I'm in my room, folks."

They had been lucky. Apparently the cops had something else to do on that day. In any case, it had been a warning. The city council wanted the squatters to sign a contract:

Self-help project, renovation with fifteen percent work contribution and after that, minimum rent. If they agreed to such a deal it meant that they would be in a legal trap. If they would not comply with every letter of the contract it would be easy for the city to throw them out.

At the moment much of the public opinion was on their side. Once they signed a contract and breached it, it would be a different story.

10.
SAFETY FIRST

They needed a new lock for the main door. Not because of the cops, the cops just used a battering ram anyway.

The new lock was simply a regular safety measure. Recently a lot of things had disappeared: Pflaume's leather jacket was gone, Meike lost seventy marks, and Kermit missed a bag of weed. Due to the fact that the lock was broken, practically anyone could enter and take whatever was accessible.

At first they had tried to pay for the upkeep of the house by themselves, but soon they were virtually bankrupt. So many things needed repair that they had to improvise.

On the way to the home improvement store, Hucky felt extremely queasy. It was a premonition. Nobody said a word. They had the windows open as their hair fluttered in the wind. Falk parked near Wittenbergplatz.

Hucky pushed the cart through the huge home improvement store, and Falk and Kugelblitz walked beside him. They stopped in front of a shelf with extension cords. Falk picked one up and did as if he was evaluating it.

"We must be careful," he said. "They are on the alert, recently."

"Sure thing," Kugelblitz replied.

Falk put the extension cord back on the shelf, and they walked on. In the middle of the aisle two sales guys set up a stand with sanders.

"One of you will cover my right, the other my left, and I'll quickly bag it, okay?" Falk hissed. Kugelblitz and Hucky nodded.

They walked up to the shelf with the cylinder locks. Nearby two Turks checked out a power drill. An associate walked through the adjacent aisle. On a monitor ran an advertising clip about anti-mold paints.

Falk suddenly turned and walked past the locks.

"What's the problem, man?" Kugelblitz asked.

"I don't know," Falk said. "Somebody is watching us. I can feel it."

"Nonsense. But if you don't have the guts..."

They stood in front of a shelf with rubber hammers. Falk took one out and hit into his hand. He acted as if he were looking for something on the shelves, occasionally looking right and left. Suddenly he froze. "I've got it ..."

He pointed to a mirror at the end of the aisle. "Behind that thing sits a guy, wanna bet?"

"So what?" said Kugelblitz. "If we shield you they don't see zilch from there."

They went back to the shelf with the cylinder locks. Hucky and Kugelblitz positioned themselves strategically, so Falk could not be seen from any angle. Falk took the lock and let it slip into the sleeve of his jacket.

They stuck around for a while and acted as if they were checking out different kinds of merchandise. Then they headed for the checkout lines.

"Somehow I got a funny feeling," Falk whispered.

"Nonsense," Kugelblitz said. "We shielded you one hundred percent."

At the register the guy in front of them paid for some nails and wooden slats. Hucky pushed the empty cart past the cash register. "Nothing?" asked the cashier. "You have absolutely nothing?"

"Nope."

Suddenly, two security guys burst through the door behind the checkout.
"Fuck," Falk said. "Let's run for it."
Hucky pushed the shopping cart towards the security guys, and the three ran towards the exit. Just before they reached it, a siren started to wail, and the sliding door snapped shut. They stumbled into each other. Hucky discovered a door with the inscription: "Parking Garage."

"This way!"

They jumped around some shopping carts pushed the door

open and ran like crazy down the stairs. Hucky tripped, almost fell, caught himself, and ran on. Right behind him the security guys. "Seal off everything," one of them shouted.

They had reached the parking deck and sprinted down the lane. Falk and Kugelblitz ran faster than Hucky, he hung back about fifteen feet. Although Kugelblitz had rather short legs, he could run like crazy. Hucky felt the security guys right behind him. He heard their footsteps, their breathing. It seemed that one of their outstretched arms could grab him at any second. How close behind were they? He could not turn around. If he did, it could cost the vital tenth of a second. He ran as he had never run before.

The parking garage was huge. Falk and Kugelblitz turned a corner. Shortly after, Hucky also turned the corner. Suddenly, directly in front of him, a car moved out of a parking spot and honked. He jumped around it and ran on as fast as he could.

Finally the exit! Was it sealed off by security? What the heck, maybe they could break through somehow. Falk and Kugelblitz were already out in the open. Hucky gave it his all. He ran past the barrier onto the street. No one was there to stop him. Only the guy in the booth gave him a puzzled look.

Two blocks further down Falk and Kugelblitz turned around a corner and stopped gasping for air. Hucky let himself drop against the wall and closed his eyes. His lungs ached, and he felt a strange pressure in his teeth.
Falk grinned. "Boy, that was close, folks, huh?"
Hucky was sweating from every pore. Kugelblitz and Falk

were completely wet as well.

They walked along a busy avenue. Traffic was heavy and moved slowly. Shoppers streamed in and out of a department store.
Falk, Hucky and Kugelblitz trotted over the crosswalk. The midday sun was at its zenith. Falk removed the lock from his sleeve and held it in the air like a trophy.

They laughed.

11.
COLORFUL BEADS

They got into the van and drove home. Falk switched into second gear. The transmission creaked.

Falk had put on his glasses. He almost never wore them, but when driving he just had to. The battered Transit attracted attention, and they were stopped quite often. Almost half of the people in the house had to wear glasses, but no one put them on. Glasses were simply uncool. It looked kind of funny when Pflaume drove the Transit. His reading glasses and the Mohawk were a fascinating combination.

Although Hucky had a driver's license, he wasn't really keen about driving. Sitting behind the wheel made him nervous, especially in congested traffic.

Hucky had passed the test in Bad Wildungen as a gift from daddy at his eighteenth birthday. He had failed the driving test at the first attempt. He had screwed up the parallel parking. It was totally embarrassing, of course. Especially since all village bumpkins had passed right away. For senior teacher von Hachenstein it was a personal humiliation that his son had failed, when all others had passed. On top of that, the additional driving lessons cost extra.

At first Hucky had not wanted to accept his father's gift.

He had only given in for his mother's sake, so the constant quarrel with daddy did not escalate any further. The fight with his father had started when Hucky was fourteen. It was the old game. The old man wanted to mold his son after himself. But Hucky was different, very different. First off all he had voted off Latin classes. Latin was crappy and of absolutely no use to him.

Hucky had chosen English and Music as majors, two things he actually was interested in, but what the hell he was to do with a Bach sonata, or with a religious canon of the Middle Ages? What he really could have used, were the riffs of "Anarchy in the UK." For hours he had been sitting in front of his tape recorder and had tried to figure out the intro.

And then there was the English teacher, Mr. Molnar. Okay, after the war he had been held in an American army prison, but he had no idea what was going on today in the East End. In the English class they read something like *Pride and Prejudice*. For the fun of it, Hucky had once asked what "Never mind the bollocks" meant. Molnar didn't know. Hucky knew it, since he had asked an English Pistols fan in Amsterdam. But he didn't tell anyone, it was his little secret. Of course he had not really won a new friend with his question, and in the next English class, the teacher punished him with icy ignorance. Probably he had researched what the phrase meant.

Quite early on Hucky had figured out that he and school did not fit together. It was a waste of time. When he received his draft letter he was in 13th grade, shortly before graduation. That same night he had secretly stuffed some clothes in a bag and had hitchhiked to Berlin.

53

Falk suddenly stepped on the brakes. Hucky and Kugelblitz toppled forward and barely managed to secure themselves to the dashboard.

"Sorry, guys" Falk said. "Just saw someone."

He set back a few feet and looked into the window of Café M. A black woman with colorful beads in her hair sat at one of the tables. She was reading a newspaper and drinking coffee.

"Just wait a second," Falk said.

He left the engine running and jumped out of the van. Hucky and Kugelblitz looked on as he chatted with the black beauty.

"Damn hot," Kugelblitz said admiringly. He did not have anything going on at the moment. He worked on Frida K. from the squat in Blumenthalstrasse, but she kept him at a distance. Falk, however, had it easy with women. When he walked into a room, you saw him instantly. He didn't even have to do anything, just stand there.

Sometimes Hucky compared himself to Falk, and with him it was a bit different, unfortunately. Hucky had to work to get noticed. And that's why he practiced for his solos like a madman. If he played a solo on stage, they all looked at him. And after that, they recognized him and slapped him on the shoulder. Even with Meike it had happened for the first time at a T.T. Embargo concert. After the show, she suddenly clung to him - Hucky's first groupie. And not only that, several other girls had looked at him quite invitingly as well. Since that moment Hucky had tasted blood.

The stage was his life.

"Hello there, gentlemen, can I see your license and registration, please?"

A traffic cop looked through the window. They stood in the second row.

"We just delivered something," Hucky said. "We're on our way home." He honked.

Falk saw the cop and jumped out of the coffee shop.

"Sorry, sorry, officer," Falk said. "We are already gone."

The cop scrutinized the battered van. "License and registration, please."

Falk fumbled his driver's license out of his pocket, and Hucky pulled the registration from the glove compartment.

The cop walked away a few steps and spoke into a radio.

Falk chewed his lower lip. He already had plenty of traffic violation points in the central registry.

The cop came back. "You are aware that you are standing in the second row, aren't you?"

"Yeah, sure, officer," Falk said. "I only briefly stepped out, and we are already gone, practically."

The cop nodded. "Where are your glasses?"

Falk had taken off his glasses to talk to the black beauty and tucked them in his shirt pocket. "Here, here they are..."

He put them on and smiled.

"Okay," said the cop. "We will turn a blind eye today."

He looked at the black girl in the coffee shop.

"We were once young as well. But next time you will be looking for a proper spot, you cannot stand in the second row, okay?" He returned license and registration.

"Yeah, sure, will do, officer. Thank you!"

Falk jumped behind the wheel and stepped on the accelerator. "Jerk," he muttered under his breath.

He pulled a piece of paper from his shirt pocket and kissed it. He had gotten her number.

"American?" Kugelblitz asked.

"No, much better," Falk said, grinning. "Venezuela. *Una mamacita muy caliente!*"

Some time ago Falk had visited a socialist youth camp in Nicaragua. That's why he spoke Spanish.

They reached home, and Falk parked the car. Lilli came running out of the house. "Did you make it?"

"Sure as hell!" Falk held out the lock.

Lilli stood on tiptoe, laid hands around Falk's neck and gave him a kiss.

12.
THE DECISION

It was cold in the community room. Kugelblitz lit the oven, using the logs cut from the railway ties. Carla juggled her rubber balls, and Meike had a cat on her lap. They all talked at once, until Kermit said, "Hey, can we start now, I want to say something!"

He leaned forward and looked at everybody individually. "I think, the general vibe in the house is damn lousy."

"Lousy?" Kugelblitz said. "Why? I think it's great."
"Can I finish, please?" said Kermit.
"Yeah, man" Lilli said. "Let him finish."
"I think it's just sad how we treat each other lately," Kermit said. "There is simply no love anymore. You walk past someone on the stairs and all you get is a mumbled 'Hey!' and that's it. This sucks, and I think it'd be better to not say anything at all."
"Ok, what do you expect from me?" Pflaume said. "Shall I hug you and caress your balls, or what?"
Kermit groaned. "You really don't get it man, you don't get it at all."
"Blah, blah, blah ..." Kugelblitz said.

Hucky went to the bathroom. Lilli had painted the toilet bowl blue. In some places the paint had flaked off. An empty train drove by. Hucky stayed in the bathroom for a moment and looked into the night. The discussion regarding the bad vibe was nothing new. It came up every month.

When Hucky went back into the community room, they were all quiet. A bus drove past and the floor trembled.
Pflaume pulled out a bottle of red wine from inside his leather jacket and took a gulp. Candy also took a gulp. She tilted her head far back, and her leather cap slid into the back of the neck. She wiped her mouth with her sleeve. "By the way, what's going on with lil' Heiner?" she said. "I thought he wanted to come by today."
"True," Falk said.
"Let me have a sip!" Kugelblitz took the wine bottle from Candy and drank. His Adam's apple bobbed up and down.

Suddenly Heiner stood in the door.

He smiled. "Evening, everyone, nobody heard me ring the bell?"
"Nah," Candy said. "Didn't hear anything."
Heiner closed the door and struck the dust of his reindeer sweater. "Not really pleasant to squeeze through that cave in the basement, that's for sure."
"Huh?" Kugelblitz said. "Was that trap door open?"
Heiner nodded.
"I'd really like to know which idiot uses the trap door and does not close it again," Kugelblitz said. "I've already said it a zillion times."
Heiner touched his head. "We need to put a lamp in that basement. I almost broke my skull."

Heiner had discovered their secret escape route. Not even the cops had found it. Heiner had crawled through a tunnel only twenty five inches high and had forced himself through a small hole in the wall. His sweater and corduroy pants were dirty.

It was eerily quiet.

"Everything okay?" Heiner said. "Anything wrong?"
Pflaume took the wine bottle from Kugelblitz and drank.
Falk opened the oven and threw in more wood.
"Everything's all right," Candy said and crossed her legs.
"Somebody else say something."
"I wanted to ask how it's coming along with the saw," Heiner said. "It's actually my friend's, and I need to return in three or four days. Do you think you'll be done by then?"
"You can take it back today," Kugelblitz said.
Heiner looked at him in astonishment. "You no longer need it?"
"We can do the rest by hand."
"But why? Three or four days would be no problem."

Another bus drove past and the floor trembled slightly.

"It won't work with the elevator here," Falk said.
"Well, sure, that it wouldn't happen overnight was clear from the get-go," Heiner said.
"No," Falk said. "I mean, we don't want one at all."
"I don't understand. Why not?"
"Isn't there any other house with an elevator already in it?" Kermit said. "Wouldn't that be easier?"
"But that's exactly the point," Heiner said. "This house is just perfect for it. There is no other like it."
"Fuck the elevator," Candy said. "The fuckin' elevator is totally irrelevant. The point is: We do not like you. Period."

59

There was dead silence.

Heiner pointed to his legs. "That's why, right?"
"This has absolutely nothing to do with it, man," Candy said.
"Sure has!" Heiner said. "It's always been like this. I just thought you might be different, maybe."
"Whatever, man," Pflaume said. "We told you now, and that's it."
"No, no, wait a minute," Heiner said. "So you two are against me, okay. How 'bout the others?"
Heiner looked around and tried to make eye contact.
Hucky dodged Heiner's glance and rolled himself a smoke.
"Nobody wants you to move in," Falk said. "It's a unanimous decision."
Heiner laughed. "Yes, yes, of course."
"It's all about fitting in, man," Falk said. "And you don't fit, here. Wouldn't it be better for you to look somewhere else?"
"I just do not understand what you have against me," Heiner said.
"That's it," Pflaume said. "That's exactly it. You just don't get it."
He put on his jacket and stood up.
"Wait," Candy said. "I'll go with you."

They all got up, and Heiner was left alone.

13.
A CAT NAMED FRITZ

Hucky probably wouldn't have noticed the cat at all, had she had not always peed right in front of his door. It stank horribly. He asked around and discovered that the cat did not belong to anyone in particular.

He tried to get rid of the smell with detergent, hoping that the cat might vanish of her own accord, but he had no luck. She always came back and peed at the same spot. Once, when he was in the kitchen making coffee, she snuck into his room and peed on his pillow. After that it was plain sailing: The cat had to go!

He lay in wait for her, grabbed her and put her in a bag. He left the zipper open a bit, so she could breathe, went to the S-Bahn station and got on the train to Lichtenrade. He wanted to release her somewhere far away.

In the S-Bahn compartment he sat opposite two grannies. One was tiny. Her legs were too short for the seats, and her feet dangled three inches above the ground. The other wore a hat with a feather. Suddenly, the cat meowed. She kept on meowing like crazy.

"Good Lord," said the granny with the hat. "Can't you take her out of the bag? This is heart wrenching!"

Hucky pulled open the zipper, and the cat stuck out her head. She jumped on his lap, he caressed her, and she purred.

"Look, how cute," said the short one.
"Yes," said the one with the hat. "A real cutie. What's her name?"
"Her name?"
"Of course. Doesn't she have one?"
"She sure does," Hucky said.
"So what is it?"
"Fritz."
"Fritz?"
"Yes, Fritz."
"So, it's a tomcat?"
"No, a female."

"A female called Fritz?"

"Yes," Hucky said. "Why not?"
The grannies looked at each other, puzzled.

Hucky caressed the cat, and she purred again.
"You want her?"
"Excuse me?" said the one with the hat. "You want to give her away?"
"Yeah. You want her?"
"No, thank you."
Hucky asked the short one. "How about you? You want her?"
"No."

At the next station the grannies got off. Hucky put the cat in the bag and got off as well. Alongside some garden plots he let Fritz out and walked away. The cat ran after him.

Hucky turned around abruptly and shooed her away. Fritz jumped back a bit, but when Hucky walked on, she followed him again. He put on a faster pace and turned around a few corners to confuse Fritz, but the cat stayed behind him.

Hucky hid behind a fence, wanting to scare Fritz when she came around the corner. Fritz did not come. He looked around the fence, and she stood five feet away, waiting.

Hucky ran as fast as he could to the S-Bahn entrance, jumped up the stairs and sat down on a bench in the middle of the platform. Apart from him, there was nobody. The wind rustled in the bushes on the embankment.

Finally, the train arrived. Hucky got in and turned around. Fritz stood on the deserted platform. She meowed. The doors slammed shut, and the train drove off. He had gotten rid of her. Surely she would find someone else who cared for her.

The next morning a strange tickling on his cheek woke him up: Fritz!

She purred.

Hucky freaked out. How was this possible? How had she found her way back? He slapped on the mattress. Fritz jumped up but settled down again three feet away. Damn, how could he get rid of her? It was totally pointless to release her somewhere, she would simply come back again. What the hell could he do?

Twenty minutes later he stood in front of the Wall. It was one of the places with graffiti and slogans. He took Fritz out of the bag and looked at her. "Okay, my friend," he said. "Take care. You'll make it somehow!" He threw Fritz in the air, and the screeching cat flew over the wall into East Berlin.

Silence.

Was Fritz hurt? That could not really be, since cats always fell to their feet. However, he had forgotten that the East had buried mines in the ground. Fritz could blow up! No, probably not. She was probably too light and could not trigger the mines. Or could she?

A few yards away there was an observation deck for tourists. Hucky climbed up and looked at the death strip, but he could not discover Fritz among the tank barriers. Maybe she was sitting directly behind the wall.

"Fritz!" he shouted. "Meow!"

Silence. Hucky remained on the observation deck for a while and waited. Behind the death strip stood a second wall which prevented the common East German to get into the security zone. Behind that second wall Hucky could get a glimpse into East Berlin. A small Trabant car of East German make rattled over the cobblestones. On a balcony, a woman hung laundry. Two girls carried shopping nets with potatoes.

Hucky had been in East Berlin only once and had no plans to go back anytime soon. It was worse than Bad Wildungen. From Bad Wildungen you could escape, at least.

A travel coach drove up. Japanese tourists climbed on the observation deck and took photos.

Fritz never came back.

14.
THE EVICTION OF BLUMENTHALSTRASSE

The alarm bell rang incessantly. Hucky ran out of his room and looked down the stairs. Kugelblitz peered up from below.

"The Blumenthal!" he shouted. "They are evicting the Blumenthal, let's go!"

Ten minutes later they were in the van, except for Falk. Nobody knew where he was, not even Lilli. Pflaume had misplaced his glasses, so Hucky had to drive.

He turned the key in the ignition. The van stuttered but eventually started. Carla and Lilli sat with Hucky on the front bench and the others on crates in the cargo area. Kermit slipped a face mask over his head, Candy put on a motorcycle helmet, and Pflaume tied a red bandana around his mouth.

Using force, Hucky shifted into first gear. Something was wrong with the transmission, but as long as the van was still running, they would not touch the engine. He maneuvered out of the parking space and turned on to Yorckstrasse.

Kermit slid a tape into the recorder and turned it on full blast. Bob Marley: "Get up stand, up, stand up for your rights ...!"

The Blumenthal was the squat to which they had the best connection, and Hucky knew almost all of them.

"The street is full of combat vans," Candy shouted through her helmet. "They sent an entire army."

Hucky stepped on it and cut the curves. The van was a scrap bowl. The steering wheel wobbled, and the brakes only worked when pumping vigorously with the pedal. It took some luck to move this clunker safely through traffic. Kugelblitz bit a piece of skin from his thumb. "Hopefully nothing happened to Frida," he said. "Hopefully the pigs won't harm her."

The traffic lights were constantly red, the streets were congested. Bob Marley blared at full volume from the tape recorder: "… get up, stand up …, don't give up the fight!"

They were stuck in a huge traffic jam. Hucky swerved and drove on the right turn lane all the way to the front. Several drivers honked angrily.

"Shut up, you morons," Hucky hollered and hit full throttle when the light jumped to green. He felt that Lilli looked at him admiringly. He had suddenly taken the lead.

Then, finally, the Blumenthal. No roadblocks, no cops, nothing. They had come too late.

The doors and windows on the ground floor were bricked up. Only the black flags were still hanging on the facade and fluttered in the wind. Kermit pulled himself up on an old sign that hung above the door. He reached a ledge and moved to a window on the second floor.

"Everything smashed in," he said. "Ovens, floors,

everything shattered!" Kugelblitz spat in the gutter. Lilli started to weep, and Pflaume gave her a hug.

Candy finally expressed what they all thought. "We need to do something, anything!"

15.
THE RIOT

They met at Kottbusser Tor. The squatters from the Blumenthal had been taken into custody. Some of them were said to be injured.

Hucky fastened the laces of his Doc Martens. He pulled up the collar of his jacket and buttoned it in front. This way he could hardly be recognized since only his eyes looked out. You could not really call it a disguise, because he was not disguised, just shielding himself from the wind.

They stood closely together. Hucky, Pflaume, and Candy, Carla and Kermit, Meike, Kugelblitz, and Lilli. The only one missing was Falk. Where the hell was he?

About three hundred people had gathered in the square next to the subway exit. Hucky knew a few of them by sight. Some held up posters. One read: "Stop Evictions!" Another: "Fat Cats, Speculators, and Imperialists out!" And a third: "Blumenthal, we loved you so much!"

Meike looked at her watch. "I have to go!" She had an inventory meeting in the health food store. If she did not show up, they would probably fire her. She hugged Hucky and gave him a kiss. "Take care of yourself, okay?"

Hucky nodded. Meike still held him and gave him a second kiss. "*Ciao*, dear."

A subway train drove in on the elevated track. Commuters streamed out of the exits. Most came from work. Some squinted suspiciously at the crowd. It was clear that there would be trouble.
Lilli was standing next to Hucky. She stared into space.
"Where is Falk?" He asked.
Lilli shrugged. "Who cares?"

Suddenly Meike was back. "Here, I forgot. You might need it!" She held an energy bar in her hand - 100% organic. Whole grains, nuts, honey. They made those in the health food store. She put it in Hucky's pocket, gave him a kiss again and squeezed out of the crowd.

The protest started moving. Some people suddenly had stones in their hands. Hucky began to feel a bit uneasy. It looked like the affair could become dicey.
They started shouting: "Stop eviction, fat cats out, stop eviction, fat cats out!" Suddenly the first stones started to fly. The window of a bank shattered to pieces. A barrage of stones rained on display windows. The crowd ran on. More and more people joined, and now there were maybe a thousand.
A barrage of stones hit the windows of a department store. Glass shattered, mannequins fell, a plastic ball rolled onto the sidewalk. The street was deserted, not a single passer-by. Behind closed curtains curious faces.

Hucky had not thrown a stone, yet. It just wasn't his thing. Suddenly Lilli stood beside him and put a large cobblestone in his hand, "Let's go, man! What are you waiting for?"
She stormed forward with a battle cry and tossed her stone into a display window. She had thrown it so vigorously that her Inca beanie had fallen off her head. She put it on again

and fastened the drawstrings under her chin. Hucky was stunned. He had not expected her to have that much strength.

They ran on. Hucky still had the stone in his hand. They stood in front of a supermarket. Lilli was right next to him. "Go on, hurry up."
Hucky weighed the stone in his hand. It was pretty heavy. If he didn't throw it now, Lilli would think he was a sissy. He took aim at the supermarket's front door and hurled the stone with all his force into the window.

"Bang!"

Hucky had smashed a hole in the door. A couple of guys broke the remaining pieces of glass from the frame and rushed into the supermarket. Lilli ran in as well and Hucky followed through.

The crowd picked items from the shelves that could easily be pocketed: Chocolate bars, cigarettes, cognac, and whiskey bottles. They worked up into a frenzy, and it was not long until shelves were overturned. Lilli grabbed a pack of chocolate biscuits. Hucky also had to take something. But what? There was no way he could get to the shelves with the spirits or cigarettes. More and more people squeezed into the supermarket, and the aisles were congested. Some Turks also squeezed in and grabbed what they could carry. Suddenly fire broke out and people started to scream.

"Let's get out," Lilli screamed. "Just get out of here."

Hucky grabbed a can of Hunter's Stew and stuffed it into

the side pocket of his jacket. It had been the only thing within easy reach. At the front door there was a bottleneck. More and more people wanted in, others wanted out. There was no getting through.

Hucky and Lilli hopped on the pedestal behind the display windows. One window was already partially broken and an advertising poster hung down in shreds. The gap in the window was too small. Hucky pulled out the can with the Hunter's Stew using it to smash more glass from the frame. Finally, the hole was big enough and they could jump into the open.

As they passed the bridge at Kottbusser Damm, Hucky could hardly believe his eyes. On the other side of the street stood Heiner with a stone in his hand. He had shaved off his beard and wore a red headband. His black hair stood up in spikes, and on his leather jacket he had painted the anarchist "circle A".

When he realized that Hucky and Lilli had seen him, he reached out and smashed his stone into a display window. He had a lot of strength in his arm, and the sound of the shattering glass was extremely loud. "Destroy, destroy!" he screamed. "Everything will fall to pieces!"

Suddenly, sirens and flashing lights.

The cops came driving up from several directions. Screeching brakes. Combat vans blocked the streets. Some guys overturned a Mercedes and set it into flames. Thick, black smoke billowed up. All of a sudden everything was burning around them and people screamed. The cops used water cannons.

There was only one escape route. Along with fifty others, Hucky and Lilli ran into a side street. A squad of cops was behind them.

"Come on, let's get in there," Lilli shouted. They tried to get into a door of a building. It was locked. The cops came closer. Hucky and Lilli ran ahead and tried the next door. This one opened, and they hurried through the corridor into the backyard. Suddenly there was a wall topped with barbed wire. They heard the cops storming into the house behind them.

Hucky made a tree ladder, and Lilli climbed up on the wall.

She clung to a pillar and pulled Hucky up. When they jumped down on the other side, Hucky sprained his foot. He cursed and limped on.
Behind them, the cops had arrived at the wall.
"Where the hell are they?"
"They must have jumped the wall!"

Lilli and Hucky ran towards the exit gate and burst out onto the street.
Only three hundred meters to the elevated subway line. Hucky's foot hurt like crazy, but he gritted his teeth and limped on. They saw a train driving up to the station.
"We must catch this one," Lilli screamed.

They ran up the stairs and arrived just in time. The doors of the subway closed behind them, and they fell against the compartment wall, panting. They spontaneously hugged each other, and Hucky felt Lilli's heart beat and her breast moving up and down when she breathed.

She was skinny and fragile. Almost like a bird.

The subway rode over a long curve. It was already dark. A few neon signs and the TV Tower in the East were glowing through the night.

16.
WINE FROM THE BOTTLE

There was a knock on the door. "Hucky ...?" Meike said. "Are you there?"

Hucky motioned Lilli to be quiet. Meike pushed down the handle. Fortunately, he had bolted the door.

"Hucky...?" Meike knocked on the door again. A moment of silence. "Strange ... I thought I heard something. Well, if you're in there, I'm in my room, okay?"

Hucky and Lilli had made love three straight times. By candlelight and with an occasional sip from the wine bottle. He didn't have any glasses in the room, and for obvious reasons it had been advisable not to go to the kitchen.

Hucky lit a cigarette and blew smoke rings into the air. He had finally made his secret desires a reality and felt that he had somehow even conquered Amanda Lear. Was this the best day of his life? Absolutely. Could Steve Jones have done a better job? Probably not.

Hucky took another sip from the wine bottle. He had grown used to the stuff, and it went down like butter.

Lilli was gentle as a lamb. She caressed his chest hair. "Didn't know you're into me," she said. "Always thought you didn't like me."

"A man grows with his tasks," Hucky said.

Lilli kept on caressing his chest. "True."
She pointed to his swollen ankle. "Better?"
Hucky nodded.

After they had arrived at home, Lilli had rubbed his ankle with ointment while looking into his eyes. Shortly afterwards it had happened. Could it be that women liked injured heroes? Pretty sure. Men definitely liked nurses, that was certain.

There was another knock on the door. "Lilli?"

This time it was Falk. How the heck did he know that she was with Hucky? Had he heard her voice? Falk knocked again. "Lilli are you in there?" Lilli wanted to answer, but Hucky held his hand over her mouth. She pulled his hand away.

"Yes, I'm here," she shouted. "And we just screwed three times in a row."

Hucky held his breath. He took another sip of wine.

"Why don't you just go back to your chocolate doll, if she's so hot and all," Lilli shouted.
Falk groaned. "I visited my grandma, dammit."
Lilli giggled hysterically. "Sure, logical, and tomorrow is Christmas ... How stupid do you think I am? I saw you, you hypocritical swine."

Falk was silent for a moment.

"Okay," he said. "All I wanted to know is if you're okay."
"I'm FAN-TAS-TIC, thank you. And now fuck off, you loser."

She buried her face in the pillow and sobbed.

17.
COUGH DROPS WON'T HELP

Hucky woke up being terribly thirsty. The spot next to him was empty. Lilli had disappeared during the night. She had forgotten her earrings on the bedside table.
He opened the curtains. A beautiful, sunny spring day. Almost summer.
He pulled the curtains shut again. The harsh light didn't do him any good. They had guzzled five bottles of red wine and smoked almost an entire packet of tobacco.

Hucky pulled on his torn jeans and limped barefoot out of his room. His left ankle was still swollen.
The house seemed deserted. Lilli's door stood open, but she was not in her room. He hobbled down to the kitchen on the second floor. Where the hell was everybody?

Meike sat in the kitchen, already dressed for work, her bag beside her. She stared out the window onto the S-Bahn premises.
"Good morning," Hucky said.

Meike remained silent.

Hucky checked out the fridge. Nothing except a half-eaten strawberry yogurt, which had two mold rings on the surface. The water canister was empty and there was no coffee, just a little sugar. Meike turned around. "Is that all

you have to say?"
Although she lived on the floor below him, she had probably heard what had happened. Or Falk had told her.

Hucky sat down at the kitchen table and rubbed his temples. His hangover was unbearable.
Meike stood up. "So it was all a big lie, huh? You lied and cheated, cheated and lied, huh?"

Hucky buried his face in his hands. It was a disaster.

Meike grabbed her bag, stormed out of the kitchen and slammed the door. A piece of plaster fell off and splashed on the battered wooden floor. Hucky grabbed the water canister and limped barefoot and shirtless across the street to the Karadeniz.

Gerlinde Steinmöller gawked out her window again. He threw her a kiss.

Ismail grinned when he saw Hucky. "Summer been already starting, yes?" Hucky took a sip of water from the tap behind the counter and filled up his canister. He dug in the pockets of his jeans. Thirty-five pfennigs. He asked if he could get a cheese patty and a coffee on credit.

"No problem, my friend." Ismail opened his notebook and made a new entry on Hucky's page. Some of the others also had a page in the book.

"We're at how much, now?"

"Fifty-seven fifty, my friend."

Hucky sipped fresh coffee and took a bite out of the cheese patty. Slowly, he felt a little better. The tea house was almost empty in the morning. Three guys sat around a table playing cards, and a Turkish radio channel ran on a world receiver.

Hucky hobbled back to the house with his canister. The spring sun shone on his face, and he narrowed his eyes.

He put the water canister down in the store and limped to the door leading to the yard. Heiner's piano still stood in one corner of the store together with the circular saw and his old bed frame.

Several cackling chickens walked around the yard. He checked the coop and also the bushes. Nothing. Someone had collected all the eggs.

Hucky put the water canister in the kitchen, fished the mold from the surface of the strawberry yogurt and ate the rest.

He filled some water in their watering can and took it to his room. He looked for a headache remedy, but couldn't find any, only cough drops. Maybe those would help. He dribbled some drops directly into his mouth. The stuff was extremely bitter, and he shuddered. Actually, the drops were supposed to be taken with sugar, but the sugar was downstairs in the kitchen. He took a deep gulp from the watering can to get the bitter taste out of his mouth.

Hucky pulled the sock with his loose change from under the mattress. One mark and twenty-three pfennigs. Along with the thirty-five pfennigs in his pants he had one mark and fifty-eight.

He rolled one and smoked. The hangover got worse immediately, and he threw the stub in the trash.

Occasionally they made some money with the van, helping somebody to move or driving debris to the dump. Or they renovated apartments. But sometimes there was nothing for weeks. Now and then, Hucky's mother sent him a hundred marks to a P.O. box, which he had set up at the central post office. Almost daily he went there to check, but for more than five weeks the box had remained empty. He had to call his mother. After all, it could be that the scoundrels from the post office had skimmed a couple of letters.

He suddenly remembered Meike's energy bar. It had to be in his pocket, still. He found it and greedily ate it.

He grabbed his guitar and played the first few bars of "Sometimes Cold, Sometimes Hot": "Living in a squat, dududu-duuh, dududu-duuh..., sometimes cold, sometimes hot, dududu-duuh, dududu-duuh ..." Somehow it sounded like crap this time. He put the guitar away.

Now, that it was all over with Meike, there loomed another problem, still. She probably would want her 250 marks back that he had borrowed. He dreaded the next community meeting. She was capable of putting the issue on the agenda.

Hucky slumped down on his mattress and pulled the blanket over his head.

18
THE INVASION OF THE KILLER BUBBLES

There was a knock on the door, and Kugelblitz peered into Hucky's room. "What's wrong, man, the Killer Bubbles are on today. It starts in two minutes."
Hucky had stayed in bed all day, sleeping or listening to BBC on his tube radio. He had forgotten that it was Sci-Fi night on Channel Three.

They watched the film on the TV set in the community room. Kugelblitz had brought over the old wing chair from the guest room, Candy and Pflaume lay together under a quilt on a mattress, and Kermit fed the stove with wood. At night it could still be quite chilly.
Hucky sat in the rocking chair. The gentle movements calmed him. He was glad that Meike was not there.

A baking sheet with apple pie stood on the table. Kugelblitz always baked pies for Sci-Fi Night. He had learned it from his grandma.
Kugelblitz took a piece and snapped some whipped cream on it. Hucky also grabbed a piece.

The film was an American B-movie: Huge soap bubbles attacked the Earth. They seemed quite harmless initially, but if you came too close to them, they burst and turned into bloodthirsty monsters.

Kugelblitz stared at the screen, wearing 3-D glasses made from cardboard. He licked whipped cream from his thumb. The killer bubbles slowly trickled down on a sleepy American town.

Kermit tapped Kugelblitz on the shoulder. "Let me have the glasses!"

Kugelblitz gave him the 3-D contraption, and Kermit adjusted the glasses on his nose back and forth. "It's not in 3-D, man."

"No, not now," Kugelblitz said. "But in the original it is."

Kermit took off the glasses. "But then they are absolutely worthless, man!"

Kugelblitz put them back on. "Anyway, I like it better that way."

Candy grabbed a piece of cake and took a big bite. "Yummy!"

A few killer bubbles turned into bloodthirsty monsters and pursued a school class. A little girl with a white ribbon in her hair ran screaming along a road. She dropped her school bag.

Pflaume drank red wine. Hucky went to the kitchen and took a glass. On the S-Bahn premises an empty train drove by. Almost all the apartments on the opposite side of the tracks had a flickering TV set. Sci-Fi Night was popular.

Hucky sat down next to Pflaume and drank red wine. The wine warmed him from within, and he immediately felt better.

In the film, more and more killer bubbles burst, and the monsters seemed to be everywhere. A young woman screamed like crazy and ran for her life. She stumbled and fell flat on her face.

"Evening, everyone." Falk and Lilli stood in the doorway.

They were holding hands.

Hucky felt as if an ice pick was being driven through his heart. Candy stifled a giggle. The others grinned as well. Everyone seemed to know about the romantic entanglements. News of this kind spread quickly.

A few minutes later Falk and Lilli left again. Hucky poured himself a second glass of red wine and drank it down in one gulp. He stared at the killer bubbles and tried to turn off any thoughts. Even a completely absurd B-movie was better than to think.

In the film, the sheriff distributed weapons and the small town folks formed a combat unit to fight the monsters.

Suddenly they heard glass shattering. Kermit turned the TV volume down, and they heard it a second time. They jumped up and ran into the kitchen.

Shards were all over the place. The skinheads had smashed the windows again. Of course, they had attacked again from the S-Bahn premises. In the dark you could barely see the cowards there.

Pflaume turned on their homemade searchlight: a 500 watt bulb in a metal bucket. He lit the bushes - no one to be seen.

"If we could only catch these assholes," Kugelblitz said.

"We should build a trap there," Pflaume said. "Would be hilarious to find them sitting down in the hole."

They kept the searchlight on, pushed the shards into a corner and went back to the community room.

85

The film was over. Because of the stupid skinheads they had missed the end.

19.
THE SEARCH

The battering ram thundered three times against the door, and the cops were in. When Hucky looked out the window, he saw the combat unit storming into the house. Someone rang the emergency bell on the second floor, but a few seconds later, the bell was silenced.

Hucky rolled a cigarette and smoked. Suddenly the door flew open and two cops with helmets stood before him. One pushed his visor up and held out his hand: "ID, please!" Hucky produced his ID.
"Do you have any illegal substances, weapons, explosives, and if so, you better tell us where they are, since we'll find them anyway."
"I am clean."
"This is not what I asked you, buddy. Answer my question."
"Okay, *nyet*."
"Listen, you wiseass. If you fuck with us, we'll fuck with you, got that?"

One cop remained in the doorway, the other rummaged through the room. He pulled open the chest of clothes, went through Hucky's papers and even crawled under his sleeping platform. He discovered the bag with the dirty underwear and reached inside. When he realized that he had caught Hucky's used briefs, he pulled his hand back quickly. The one who had the ID, went down to the police car, the other remained in the doorway making sure Hucky wouldn't disappear.

Hucky took his guitar and started to play a few riffs, but the cop motioned to him to stop it.
"Can I turn on the radio at least?"
"*Nyet.*"
Hucky grinned. The cop had a sense of humor.

In the days after the disaster with Lilli, Hucky had come down with a severe case of the blues. Once he had even stood on the tall railway bridge and stared down at the tracks. But then, the sun broke through the dense cloud cover and dipped the S-Bahn premises in a surreal light.
The whole day had been cloudy and gray and just at that moment the sun broke through? Was this a sign? A divine hint that his mission was not yet finished? Hucky suddenly had an inspiration.
He hurried back home, grabbed his guitar and sat down on their roof garden. In less than half an hour, he had composed a heart-wrenching ballad: "Crying is not worth it!" And not only that. After a bottle of red wine and a few puffs he had even come up with two other songs: "My Cat Fritz" and "Nothing in the Box."

In "Nothing in the Box" he had tried his hands at a Ska beat, while "My Cat Fritz" was just straight, classic punk. He had already rehearsed all three songs with Kugelblitz. Especially "Nothing in the Box" really killed it, since Kugelblitz had come up with a brilliant bass line, counterpointing Hucky's Ska riffs. And when Hucky sang "Nothing in the box, ha, ha ..." Kugelblitz replied in falsetto style. "So what, so what ..." This was top of the line, and Hucky could not wait to test the song before an audience.

The cops had found nothing and had bolted, and the squatters were sitting in the kitchen on the second floor. Meike said they had even searched her empty cat food cans and dug through her flower pots. In Kermit's room they had found the bong. The cops had been really fast, and there was no time to disassemble it. But a bong alone didn't mean anything. You could also use it to smoke perfumed tobacco, as with any other hookah. Nevertheless, the cops had taken the bong for analysis.

Kermit went to the fridge, and took a bag of weed out of the cream cheese.

Pflaume laughed. "Sheer brilliance!"

The search did not bode well. If they were lucky, it had only been routine, if not, their days were counted.
Hucky looked toward Meike, but she avoided his glance. She had stopped speaking to him and had never mentioned the 250 marks.

20.
THE DISEASE

Frida K. from the Blumenthal suddenly had yellowish eyes. She was feeble and could barely get out of bed. The others from the Blumenthal had squeezed into other houses but Frida hadn't found anything, so they had let her move in. Especially, of course, to the delight of Kugelblitz who was still hoping to get a shot at her.

Frida K. set up an artist's studio in the attic. There she lived and worked and received occasional guests to discuss modern painting. Her artist's name was "Amparilla," but absolutely no one - except for Kugelblitz - called her that. Someone in the Blumenthal had named her Frida K. because she had grown-together eyebrows, and the moniker stuck.

As Frida suddenly became ill, she dramatically lost weight and looked even frailer than she already was. Meike had tried to get her back on her feet with a few remedies from the health food store, but she was getting worse. Finally, they heaved her into the van, and Falk drove her to the hospital.

Two days later they received the diagnosis. Some form of jaundice, supposedly highly infectious. Whether you had been infected would only become obvious after three weeks, and so they sat on a time bomb. If one of them had it, he could gradually infect all the others. The hospital had passed on the issue to the health department, so now it had become a matter of Disease Control. If the officials did not like what was going on in the house, they probably would be quarantined.

They formed several cleaning teams: Falk, Carla, and Kugelblitz scrubbed the floors, Pflaume, Hucky, and Candy cleaned up the kitchen and threw away the stuff that was scattered in the hallways, and Meike wiped the windows. Lilli painted over the walls in some places. She had the stupid habit of spray painting her thoughts. Over the sink she had written: *I peel the onion until it weeps!* On the fridge: *Empty, gotcha!* And next to her door it read: *Who you looking at? Look at yourself!* In the beginning that was kind of funny, but as a result almost all the walls were spray painted with Lilli's wisdoms, and everything looked somewhat filthy.

They kept on cleaning for hours, and in the end the house was spick-and-span. They had scrubbed the sink with steel wool, brushed the toilet bowls with a heavy duty chlorine solution and had even disinfected the door handles. And for the first time, everybody had clean fingernails at once. Anyway, they could not transform a decrepit old building into a new one, and they were scared that their effort was perhaps in vain.

But the story turned out quite differently: The Disease Control guys were pretty cool. Only two of them showed up, and they did not really scrutinize anything. They just treated the bathrooms with a special disinfectant and said that each new case should be reported immediately. But when they whispered "Do not panic, and keep it to yourselves" and didn't even want to shake hands when leaving, the squatters became slightly concerned. They looked in the health dictionary that Kugelblitz had received from his granny, and under jaundice it read at the end: "... may in some cases lead to death."

The following days were hell. All were scared that they might have it. Some thought of simply running away, but where to? And if you had it, running away wouldn't do any good anyway. You would just take it with you. So they waited and hoped for the best.

Hucky stood in front of the mirror at least twenty times a day and checked whether he could spot something yellow in his eyes. At first, everything was okay, but then it seemed that there was a faint yellow veil covering his eyes. Was this really yellow or just a bit dull? He felt around his body and checked the lymph nodes. Actually, the lymph nodes in the groin area were a bit swollen and hurt a little when touched. Were these the first signs?

He ran down to Kugelblitz's room, pulled the health dictionary off the shelf and looked under jaundice symptoms. Sure enough: Swollen lymph nodes in conjunction with yellow eyes were a dead giveaway. He couldn't believe it. He shut his eyes and felt around the groin area. Were the damn nodes swollen, or was it perhaps supposed to be this way? Why was there a slight pain when he touched them? He looked in the mirror and examined his eyes again. No, they weren't really yellow. Maybe just a bit, but that was probably normal. He pressed his index finger against his cheek. There was also a slight pain. Maybe the lymph nodes had to hurt a little when pressed? Maybe it had to be this way?

Suddenly Kugelblitz stepped in. He grinned. "Something wrong?"

"Nope," said Hucky. "Why should something be wrong?"

"Just asking" Kugelblitz said. "My room seems pretty popular lately."

"Popular?"

"They all borrow the dictionary. Pflaume came by three times already. Think you caught it?"

"Me? Why? Do I look like it?"

"Well, no idea, but you never know."

"True," said Hucky. "You never know."

"If only it wouldn't be so dangerous," Kugelblitz said. "Honestly, I think it's better if we don't touch each other for a while."

"Do you?"

"It sure would be safer."

Kugelblitz pulled out a huge pack with disposable plastic gloves.

"Just bought those. The others all use them already. Want some?"

"You think that makes a difference?"

"Well, sure. They are absolutely sterile."

"Okay," Hucky said. "Then I'll take some."

Kugelblitz gave him a pack of one hundred.

The following days they did everything with plastic gloves. They ate with plastic gloves, went to the bathroom with plastic gloves, slept with plastic gloves. One week passed, and since nobody got sick, they relaxed a bit.

But then it happened after all. They sat in the kitchen at dinner, when Lilli suddenly stood in the door, dead pale. She swallowed and said: "I think I've got it."

She'd had abdominal pain all day, felt like throwing up, and had a high fever. She was sweating like crazy and took off the Inca beanie. Her hair was greasy, the skin pale and blotchy, her eyes without luster.

They all stood in her room when Kugelblitz pulled up her eyelids and pointed a flashlight into her eyes. He had strapped a round doctor's mirror to his head. The devil knows where he got the mirror, but that was typical of him. Sometimes he came up with things that you would never expect. He flipped down the mirror and peeped through the small round opening into Lilli's eye.
Falk leaned down to Kugelblitz. "Speak up," he said.
Kugelblitz chewed on his lower lip. He leaned in closer with the flashlight.
"Spit it out," Falk said. "Did she catch it?"
Kugelblitz sat up straight again and shrugged. "Hard to say. There's nothing yellow, that's for sure."

It was a matter of conscience. If they took her to the hospital they ran the risk that the house would be evacuated. They decided that Lilli should decide for herself. She coughed and said with a meek voice. "Let's hang on."

Her condition was getting worse through the night. She had fever dreams and rolled back and forth. Kermit and Carla were at her side and stood guard, and the others sat in the kitchen and smoked.
"Dammit, I'll take her to the hospital," Falk said.
"Let's not rush it," Kugelblitz said. "Let's wait until tomorrow morning."
"She's got it," Falk said. "I know."
"A few hours won't make any difference," Pflaume said.
"But Lilli is damn sensitive. She's just like a fragile flower."
"And that's why we should let her sleep in peace," said

Pflaume. "According to my granny, a good night's sleep and a footbath cure everything. Only until tomorrow, okay?"

Hucky went up to his room. On the stairs he met Meike. She wore her hair up behind the ears, now, and the spring sun had given her a healthy tan. She apparently had lost some weight and looked damn good.

Hucky tried a smile, but Meike ignored him and walked past.

21.
THE DREAM

Hucky dreamed he was flying through a medieval landscape. He had angel wings on his back and in front of his belly hung a lute and a small knapsack. He flew over fields and meadows, rivers and lakes. Beside him fluttered butterflies, a deer jumped from a forest.

Suddenly he saw a castle in the distance and smoke rising up. It seemed like there was a feast. Being hungry, he flapped his wings a little faster. He arrived just in time. In the courtyard, a wedding party was being held.

Hucky landed and mingled with the crowd. He positioned himself next to the grill fire, and sang to the lute. He started with the song in which a country boy fell in love with a goat. It was a surefire formula, and people started to laugh. While he played, a damsel fed him grilled pieces of meat, another put a cup of wine to his lips. But Hucky only had eyes for the bride. He suspected a stunning beauty under her veil.
He had caught her attention with his song, and the bride suddenly lifted her veil. He froze. It was Amanda Lear. No, it was Lilli.
Then the groom came out of the crowd, and Hucky almost fainted. It was Falk.

At once all were silent and stared at Hucky.

"Where did he come from?" hissed Falk. "Did he come from the South?"

Suddenly a damsel dressed all in black came out of the crowd. It was Meike. "I saw him from the tower. He came in from the South, the singing bard. He brings the BLACK DEATH!"

An outcry went through the crowd. Women and children scurried away. Some of the men grabbed sticks, and Falk drew his sword.

Hucky leapt up and wanted to spread his wings, but he didn't have them anymore. He had no choice but to run, the crowd just a few steps behind him. The castle gate was closed, the only open door led into a tower. Hucky ran up the spiral stairs. Behind him he heard the bloodthirsty mob.

Finally he arrived at the lookout. It was a bright summer day, and he could see for miles in all directions - a breathtaking view. Should this be his last? Hucky checked for his wings again - nothing. The crowd reached the top. Falk stood in front with his drawn sword.

Hucky had no choice but to jump, with or without wings. He dove with a battle cry from the castle tower and fluttered his arms wildly, hoping that this would keep him in the air - without success. He darted down like a sack of paving stones. But strangely enough, he did not hit the ground. He fell and fell, but did not reach the ground. He tried to scream but couldn't. Something strangled his throat. No air!

Hucky woke up drenched in sweat. He came up and took a deep breath. Luckily it had been only a dream.

He heard voices in Lilli's room and walked over. She sat up in bed and spooned some gruel. Kermit, Carla, and Kugelblitz stood at the window.

Kugelblitz spread his arms. "False alarm," he said. "Just an upset stomach."

22.

THE ULTIMATUM

Falk could not stand still and paced nervously back and forth in the community room. "I can't believe it," he said. "How did Atze get wind of it?"

Candy threw her arms in the air. "He's buddies with some politician, what the heck do I know."

Atze was a left leaning lawyer for Tommy Weissbecker Haus. He had contacts up to the city council and usually knew first when something was cooking. He had heard that they would be evicted. There was even a court order.

"But when?" asked Falk.

Candy shrugged. "Next week, the week after next ... In any case this month."

"Those bastards," Falk said. "That guy from Youth and Sports always told me that everything is fine. He totally fooled us."

Hucky knew that it was serious this time.

"We must beat our drum," Falk said, "That's our only chance."

They printed two thousand posters that read: "Looking for a twenty-room apartment," then came a photo on which they all stood on the balcony and waved, and below it said: "Concert against Eviction."

Hucky, Kugelblitz, and Pflaume glued the posters to the

99

Yorck bridges. They climbed onto the S-Bahn premises and stuck the posters to the bridge railing, always five side by side. Pflaume held one of the posters in front of him and grinned. "Each time I look at the photo, I notice again how handsome I am."

"It's because you have a classic profile," Kugelblitz said.

"True." Pflaume nodded and pursed his thick lips.

They stood at a crossing and hung their posters on a construction fence. Hucky startled. Heiner sat in one of the passing cars. He was wearing the red headband again and the leather jacket.

"Did you guys notice Heiner in that car?" Hucky said. "He has looked at our poster."

"Sure," Pflaume said. "Why not, let him look."

Hucky said that he had seen the guy at the riot and that he had even thrown a stone. Could it be that he was a well-disguised snitch?

"Are you kidding me," Pflaume said. "No way this guy is a snitch, man. He's a mere asshole, that's what he is."

23.
THE CONCERT

"How's the light?" Kermit shouted.
Falk blinked and shielded his eyes - "A bit garish."
Kermit stood on a ladder and changed the position of the lamp, which he had attached to the ceiling of the store. It was the bucket with the 500-watt lamp. He fiddled with a few clothespins, wire, and greaseproof paper to soften the light. Of course, they had no money for decent lighting and therefore only the middle of the stage was well lit and the rest kind of faded into black.

But that was better than nothing.

Next to the entrance they had built a bar. They sold beer and vodka at friendly prices.

"One, two, one, two ..." Falk tested the PA. "How do I sound, Kerm?"
Kermit sat at the mixing desk and gave the thumbs up. He was the band's technician. He soldered cables, fixed the amps and mixed the PA. The sound system belonged to Falk and was his pride and joy. It wasn't really professional, but good enough for smaller rooms. The mics were set up at the front of the stage. In the middle stood Falk, flanked by Hucky and Kugelblitz. Behind them sat Pflaume on drums. He had no mic, since his Swabian accent came through even in English.

The squatters were sitting on the side benches waiting for television, radio and the press to show up. They had called several media outlets and even sent out a press release.

Hucky plugged his guitar into the amp and made a sound check. He played the first few notes of "Sometimes Cold, Sometimes Hot": "Living in a squat, dududu-duuh, dududu-duuh..., sometimes cold, sometimes hot, dududu-duuh, dududu-duuh ..." The others immediately sang along as they knew the song of course. The sound was okay, and Hucky switched off the amp. He didn't want to use up his powder too fast.

Today was by far the most important day in his career, and maybe it even meant his big break. He had never been on television. Not even on the radio. There was only one small newspaper article in which T.T. Embargo was honorably mentioned, as they were performing together with other bands on a neighborhood festival. Proudly, Hucky had sent the newspaper clip to his mother. He was pretty sure that senior teacher von Hachenstein had read the article and had blushed when he reached the sentence: "... particularly Hacki, T.T. Embargo's guitarist, convinced with intelligent rhythms and crystal-clear solos - a name to be remembered."

Unfortunately they had written his name in German phonetics, which had wounded him down to the bone, but thankfully it was still clear who they had meant. Hucky thought internationally and therefore wrote his nickname phonetically in English. Hopefully it wouldn't take too long until the press got it right.

T.T. Embargo was a slightly strange formation. The band had been founded by Falk and Pflaume about two years ago, and at first they had played with two guys from Ufa-Fabrik, but it just didn't fly. Exactly at that time Hucky had appeared out of nowhere while looking for a place to stay, and it had come to the magical "Message in a Bottle" session with Pflaume and Falk.

After Hucky had moved in, he had taught Kugelblitz how to play bass, and T.T. Embargo evolved into an in-house band. The problem was that Falk had no songs of his own and could only play cover versions. His favorite songs were such old chestnuts as "Locomotive Breath" and "Satisfaction" and on top of that he played the flute, an instrument that Hucky duly despised. But what could he do as he had to somehow cope with Falk. So they had reached a compromise. Fifty percent of their repertoire were cover songs, for which Falk was the lead singer and Hucky and Kugelblitz sang background, and fifty percent were Hucky's songs in which Falk also sang the lead and Hucky and Kugelblitz background.

There was one exception: "Sometimes Cold, Sometimes Hot." That was Hucky's signature song in which he sang the lead and Falk did background while shaking a tambourine and smoking a cigarette. Hucky knew that Falk felt extremely uncomfortable during this song, but under no circumstance would Hucky budge.

"Sometimes Cold, Sometimes Hot" belonged entirely to him.

At nine there was still no press, no radio, and no television. "Assholes," Falk said.

Hucky was extremely disappointed as well. Secretly he had hoped that maybe a few takes of "Sometimes cold, sometimes hot" would air on TV.

But at least they could count on the community. Shortly after nine the first people trickled in, and twenty minutes later the room was packed. Squatters from other houses, punks, and a few hippies. Also Tarik and Ismail from the Karadeniz and even the two grannies from the second-hand store where they had once bought the sheets for their flags. So many people had come that not all fit into the store, and some had to stand out on the street.

Suddenly, two photographers appeared. They took pictures with flash lights, which gave the event an official character.

Hucky was nervous. What if he blew it on stage? He had strong stage fright before every gig.
He spotted a woman with bright red, asymmetrical hair, who wrote something in a notebook. That had to be a journalist. Should he speak to her?
"Hello," he said, holding out his hand. "I'm Hucky of T.T. Embargo. Any questions ...?"
The journalist looked at him dismissively and left his hand hanging in the air. Hucky blushed. The woman had somehow implied that he wanted to compromise the freedom of the press. He had an inkling that she would probably not mention him favorably, if at all.

Falk jumped on stage and tapped on the mic. The murmur quieted down. Hucky quickly made his way to the small wardrobe that they had set up right behind the stage. The others were already there. Pflaume drummed his sticks on a chair, and Kugelblitz played a few dry runs on his bass.

They had decided that there should be no long speech.

Speeches sucked.

Falk threw his right fist straight into the air. "Resistance forever, eviction never!"
The crowd roared and some also raised their fists in the air. "Resistance forever, eviction never!"

Photo flashes clicked.

"All right, guys," Falk shouted. "Let the games begin."
Carla lowered the makeshift curtain, and T.T. Embargo climbed onto the stage. Falk gave the beat with his index finger, and they played the intro to "Locomotive Breath": "Bu, bu, bu, buu, buu, bummmmm ..." The curtain went up, the crowd roared, and Falk began to sing: "In the shuffling madness ..., of the locomotive breath ..."

Falk took the mic from its holder and jumped like a hobgoblin around the stage. He had copied this from Ian Anderson. His clothes were also similar to those of Anderson - it was a kind of Robin Hood Outfit: Suede pants, a suede vest and a hat, pointed in front and in the back.

Hucky had learned "Locomotive Breath" from a record. He had just played the song over and over and tried with his guitar until he got it right. The result was not bad, but not quite like the original. But one could clearly recognize the song, and that was all that mattered. Falk's flute solo was not like that of Anderson either and was much shorter, but it worked, somehow.

Of course they did not just let "Locomotive Breath" fade away, but played a professional, seamless transition to "Nothing in the Box." Even Falk had liked Hucky's new song right away, since the Ska rhythm suited him.
He danced rhythmically to Hucky's razor sharp syncopations, waved his long arms back and forth and sang: "Nothing in the box, ha, ha ...," and Hucky and Kugelblitz piped in falsetto style "... so what, so what ...!"

The hall was a heaving, roaring crowd. Some of the punks in the front row danced pogo and shoved each other back and forth. Hucky was in his element, and the stage fright was gone. They had made it. The audience was theirs!
Hucky played the Ska riffs cool, calm, and poised. Soon his solo was to come up, and then he stood in the spotlight, and all looked only at him.

Where was the redhead?

He discovered the journalist behind the counter. She scribbled something on her pad and did not even look at the stage. Very well. Just before the solo he would rip open the volume, and then she would certainly look at him.
The last bar before the solo. Hucky elegantly cranked up the volume, took a step forward into the light and closed his eyes.

But then, BANG! - a fuse blew. Everything went pitch black, and the music faded. Only Pflaume drummed on for a moment.

The crowd groaned disappointedly. The power failure could have been a total mood killer, but they were lucky.

Carla was supposed to juggle later in the show, so she jumped onto the stage, lit her torches and let them circle in the air. Instantly, the room lit up again, and a murmur went through the crowd. It was magical.

Only for Hucky it was damn annoying. Why did this crap happen right before his solo?

Kermit ran down to the basement to check the fuses, and Candy brought a few candles from the kitchen on the second floor. Pflaume improvised a rhythm to the flying torches, and Falk played his flute.

Hucky ran down to the basement. Without juice the show was over for him.
Kermit held a candle in front of the fuse box. He scratched his dreadlocks. "The main fuse is gone."
"Do we have a spare?" Hucky asked.
Kermit laughed.
"Can't you use one of the others?"
"The others are individual fuses, man, they are much weaker and will blow immediately."
Kermit's expression was tense. Hucky had never seen him like this.

Hucky was desperate. "Anything we can do?"

"Well, there would be one possibility, yes."
"Which would be ...?"
Kermit pointed to a thick cable that led from the top into the fuse box. "An open heart surgery."
"Huh?"
"I'll make the connection directly, without a fuse."
"Is there a risk?"

107

Kermit looked at Hucky as if he was from another planet. Hucky had no idea about electricity, and he didn't really care, he just wanted his amp to work again.

"We only have a chance if everything else in the house is turned off," Kermit said. "Everything except the things in the store."

Hucky ran upstairs. Kugelblitz stood on stage and held his Sci-Fi reading. He wore a futuristic helmet with a spiral antenna. Carla lit his manuscript with a torch.

"The Gork pulled out his laser pistol, and Rick knew that he had to re-stabilize his electrons shield, otherwise he was done for. The Gork fired, and Rick jumped to the rear hatch. His heart was pounding. Faster, damn it, he thought, faster!"

Hucky ran to the kitchen on the second floor and pulled out the plug of the fridge. He hurried through the house and pulled all the cables from the power outlets. When he got back downstairs, he also turned off the freezer. The beer would stay cold for a while anyway.

Meanwhile, Carla played "Imagine" on Heiner's piano. "Imagine there's no heaven ... it's easy if you try ..."

Some people sang along, even the redhead. The punks in the front row didn't sing along. They sat on the floor, seemed a bit bored and let a bottle of schnapps pass around.

Hucky couldn't believe his eyes when he suddenly noticed Heiner sitting among the punks, taking a swig from their bottle. Where the hell did he suddenly come from, and how did he know the punks? Screw it, it did not matter. All that mattered was the concert.

Hucky ran down to the basement again. Carla could only play that one song, and when she was finished, they had no program anymore. If the juice did not come back soon, the party would dissolve.

Hucky held the candle, and Kermit fumbled with the wires using two insulated pliers. He had put on his glasses, wore rubber boots, and plastic gloves. He almost looked like a surgeon, now, that is, a surgeon with dreadlocks. Along the wall darted a rat.

"Tape!" Kermit said.

Hucky put the candle on a ledge, tore a piece of tape with his teeth and held it out to Kermit. Suddenly sparks flew and there was a loud bang, which blew out the candle.

Darkness.

From above Carla could be heard: "Imagine there's no countries ..., it isn't hard to do ..."

Hucky lit a match. Kermit sat on the floor, stunned and still with pliers in hand. "Jesus H. Christ," he said. "That was close."

"What happened?"

"I don't know, man. I must have touched the wrong wire." Kermit rose up again. "If you can keep those two wires here side by side, then I can pull it off."

"Any risk?"

Kermit grinned. "In principle, no ..."

Hucky felt a bit queasy. He carefully took the first wire and held it in position.

"Wait," Kermit said. "You better wear those." Kermit took off his rubber boots and Hucky put them on. They were

warm and humid, and a bit too small.
Carla sang the last verse: "... you may say, I'm a dreamer ..., but I'm not the only one ..."

Hucky grabbed the first wire, then carefully grabbed the second and held them up.
"Brilliant," Kermit said. "Now bring them very close together."
Hucky held the two wires side by side, and Kermit connected them with a quick twist of the pliers.

Suddenly, the bulb in the basement lit up again and from above they heard cheers.

Hucky ran upstairs. The Fender Reverb had already begun with a feedback, because he had left the guitar leaning against the amp. He jumped on stage and went directly from the feedback into the intro of "Satisfaction." - "Bu, buu, bu, bu, buuu..., bu, bu, bu, bu, bu ...".

Falk grabbed the mic and sang: "I can't get no, oh, no, no, no ..."

It was incredibly muggy in the room and Hucky was sweating. They were all sweating. The punks danced pogo again, shoving each other back and forth. Satisfaction was not really a punk song, but it always worked. Especially after a bottle of schnapps.

Heiner was suddenly in the middle of the pogo punks. Not a small feat, considering his legs. In addition, he was obviously drunk. He tumbled back and forth, but somehow he did not fall, somehow they caught him again and again. Heiner seemed to enjoy it. From the top of his voice he sang along. "I can't get no ... oh, no, no, no ..."

Falk threw his hat away and tore the suede vest from his chest. Then he even took off his shoes and threw them into the crowd. He bounced barefoot across the stage and shouted: "Ah, hey, hey, hey, that's what I say ..."

The place was a madhouse. Pflaume briefly stopped drumming, tore off his shirt and threw it into the crowd. Hucky wanted to take off his shirt as well, but he couldn't. He would have had to stop playing, and the song would have been ruined. But suddenly one of the punk girls from the front row jumped onto the stage, ripped Hucky's T-shirt from his chest and kissed him.

A French kiss.

The crowd roared. Hucky was in his element. That was Punk, that was Rock 'n Roll. Could there be anything better in the world? Never! - Falk screamed again into the mic: "I can't get no, oh no, no, no ..."

Suddenly the sound of the PA was gone. Although Falk continued singing like a madman, he could no longer be heard. Four cops stood next to the mixer. They had turned off the PA. The band stopped playing.
The cops walked up to the stage, greeted by loud boos.
"Step down," one of the cops said: "All four of you to the squad car."

Three police cars with flashing lights stood in front of the house. Hucky glanced up to Gerlinde Steinmöller. As always she lurked out her window.

"Who's the leader here?" the chief asked.

"We all are," Falk said. He was still barefoot and wore no shirt. Hucky and Pflaume were also bare chested, and Kugelblitz was still wearing his helmet with the spiral antenna.

"Okay," the chief said. "Then to you all: It's obvious you have no permission for the event. It's also obvious you already have quite a long record in our files."

All four grinned. Hucky discovered Heiner in the vacant lot next to the house. He leaned against a wall as he threw up.

"Listen up, my friends. We have two options. Either you immediately stop any and all activities, or we will have to take you to the station. Did I make myself clear?"

"Pity," Falk said. "Just when we got the joint jumping."

"I warned you," the chief said. "If we have to come back, it will get serious. We're dealing with an unannounced event, disturbing the peace, disorderly conduct, and disobeying police orders. Are we clear?"

"Yes, Sir!" Falk said. He clicked his heels and gave him the hand salute against the forehead.

"Let's see who will have the last laugh, Woody Woodpecker," the chief said. "As far as I know, there's already a court order for your little pad. In two weeks your antics will come to an end, Mr. Funny Pants."

24.
SMOG

As Hucky opened his curtain in the morning, it was dark and hazy. He could barely see the house across the street.
He turned on the radio. After a few minutes they broadcast an announcement: Smog alert. The air currents had stalled over Berlin, and the pollution didn't disperse.
A truck drove past, its headlights casting long streaks in the fog. The neon sign from the chicken grill was only a faint red dot.

Hucky went downstairs. It was spooky as he could barely see ten feet ahead. Bus service was suspended, as was always the case with smog.
He walked to the phone booth next to the chicken grill, threw in a few coins and dialed his sister's number. It rang a long time. Someone finally answered. It was Heidi's husband, a young pharmacist, not really on Hucky's wavelength. They exchanged a few pleasantries, then Heidi came to the phone.
"Are you still alive, Holger? Mom has almost worried herself to death because you never call. And you also stopped writing. You could have at least called for mom's birthday."
Hucky bit his lower lip. Dammit, how could he have forgotten? He changed the subject and talked about the smog. "We have seen it on the news," Heidi said. "Terrible. Really, really terrible. How can you live like this?"

In Bad Wildungen there was no smog of course. According to stats from the national weather service, Bad Wildungen had among the best air quality in the nation. And the tap water was cleaner than the bottled one from the supermarket.

"Only have a few coins," Hucky said. "Can you call mom and ask her to come over?"
Hucky hung up and went into the chicken grill. It smelled of old frying grease. Bottles of hard liquor were lined up on a shelf. In a corner two guys were drinking beer and schnapps. The jukebox played *Ein Bett im Kornfeld*, a cheerful pop song about making love inside a wheat field.

Hucky bought a bottle of beer and went out again. He had to wait in front of the booth, so that he could hear the phone ring. Almost every phone booth could receive calls. The number was on the info plate. To block incoming calls, specialists of the German postal service had replaced one of the digits with a letter, but it was not particularly difficult to figure out the missing number.

The air reeked, almost like a foul-smelling soup. Hucky lit a smoke anyway. Suddenly, Kugelblitz appeared out of the smog. He had a few coins in hand. "Need to call granny."

The phone rang. Hucky went into the booth and answered. It was his mother.
"Just so you know, Holger, we still keep your room for you. It is exactly as you left it."
"Thanks, mom, but you can give it to Helge."
His mother suddenly sobbed. Hucky looked outside. Kugelblitz drank a beer.

115

"Just one question," Hucky said. "You didn't send any money lately, did you?"

"Where will this all end, Holger, that's what I am wondering. Where will it end, explain this to me."

"I only ask because there are some real scoundrels at the post office, mom. So you didn't send anything since March, right?"

"It can't go on like this, Holger. If your dad knew I am talking to you now ... How could you do this to us?"

"I'm totally fine, mom, couldn't be better. Don't need any money, really. It's all awesome."

"All awesome? You disappear in the middle of the night without saying a word, you drop out of high school, and you even forget your own mother's birthday. Is this what you call AWESOME?"

"Did you get the newspaper clip, mom?"

"Yes."

"So?"

"Dad tore it apart."

"Before you read it?"

"No, later."

"Have you read the last sentence?"

"I have."

"So?"

"How do you imagine your future, I wonder. It can't go on like this, Holger. And please don't tell me that you participated in these horrible riots. We have seen it on TV. It's just awful."

"That was a legitimate protest, mom. You can't put up with everything."

His mother blew her nose.

"You're so far away, Holger. When are you coming back?"

Hucky took a deep breath.

Kugelblitz toasted him with his beer and grinned.

"There is already a line waiting behind me, mom, I have to go."

"When shall we meet again?"

"Maybe in a few weeks in Kassel," Hucky lied. "We are planning a tour with the band."

"Really?"

"I love you, mom, but I have to hang up now."

His mother sobbed. "Promise me that you will never again take part in these terrible riots. Promise me that."

Hucky crossed his fingers. "I promise."

25.
HEINER'S OFFER

"Unbelievable," Falk nervously paced up and down in front of the window. "I wonder how he pulled it off."
"He knows some city council guy," Meike said. "And that guy has pushed it through. Now it's practically up to us."
"Something's wrong with this, folks," Candy said. "Something smells fishy, for sure."

They had called a special meeting and sat in the community room. Heiner had appeared at the health food store where Meike worked and had made a strange offer: an integrated youth project for people with special needs.

"What the hell is it with this project, exactly?" Kugelblitz asked. "I don't get it."
Meike shrugged. "Well, he's gonna move in, and maybe two or three guys like him. Something like that."
"I'm against," Pflaume said.
"Why?" asked Falk.
"'Cause it sucks, that's why."
Kugelblitz scratched his head. "Well, I mean, I don't like it either, but if it's our only chance."
"When is it supposed to start?" Falk asked.
"Well, pretty much immediately, I think," Meike said. "First, Heiner would come in and then the others a bit later. We would get renovation money, disabled-friendly toilets and a water connection, of course."

118

"I'm still against," Pflaume said.

Candy crossed her legs. "Me too."

"The guy is really something," Kermit said. "I wonder why he's not here today."

"Well, he wants us to think about it in peace," Meike said. "He says he does not want to get on our nerves."

Pflaume laughed. "He's such a sweetheart."

"Okay," Falk said. "Let me have a piece of paper."

Lilli tore a sheet from her notepad. She had scribbled on the pad during the entire meeting. It was full moon again. Falk tore the sheet into smaller pieces for a secret ballot. Who was in favor should write YES, who was against NO. Hucky took a drag on his cigarette and blew smoke rings into the air. He wrote YES on his ballot, folded it up and threw it in a cookie tin, which they passed around.

After all had thrown in their ballot, Falk shook the tin, tipped it around and counted. "One YES," he said and made a dash on Lilli's notepad. He went on counting: "YES, NO, YES, NO, NO, YES, NO, NO."

It stood four to four. One more ballot remained in the box. Falk opened it and raised his eyebrows. "LOLLYPOP? Who the hell wrote LOLLYPOP?"

Lilli giggled.

Falk rolled his eyes. "Every full moon it's the same with you for crying out loud. Are you in favor, or not?"

Lilli shrugged. "Whatever."

"Fuck the secret ballot," Falk said. "Who was in favor and who against?"

"Wait a minute," Kermit said. "Secret ballot is secret ballot. I think it should remain secret."

"Okay," Falk said. "Kerm voted against, who else?"
Of course, it was clear that Pflaume and Candy had voted against, but who was the fourth NO?
"I'm also against," Carla said. "The guy is simply annoying."

Falk moaned loudly.

"I think you still don't get it," he said. "This is about do or die, man, and not about whether you love the guy or something."
"Sure. The question is merely - if at all - where will he be?" Kermit said. "I certainly don't want him next to me."
"Me neither," said Carla.

26.
THE POWER DRILL

Two days after the special meeting, Heiner had moved in. They had given him the guest room on the second floor next to the community room and the kitchen. He did not have any direct neighbors this way.

Heiner stood in Hucky's door. He renovated his room.
"Do you know where the drill is, maybe?"
"Did you check with Kugelblitz?" Hucky asked.
"Yes."
"How 'bout with Falk?"
"He told me to ask you."
"Well, then I don't know."
"But you guys do have a drill, don't you?" Heiner said. "Then it must be somewhere."
"Yeah, right," said Hucky. "It sure is somewhere."
"Okay, but where?"

They had most of the essential tools in the squat, but whoever needed an item, just took it. Unfortunately tools hardly ever were returned to where they belonged. Sometimes you found a note: "Scissors with Carla!" or "Heater at Falk's!" or "Hatchet on the second floor!" But mostly the items were just gone, and you had to guess where they might be. They had argued endlessly over this issue and had implemented a ground rule that you absolutely had to leave a note whenever you took anything.

121

The only problem was that hardly anybody followed it.

"I don't get it," Heiner said. "That just sucks."
"Yeah, sure," said Hucky. "But that's the way it is. You just have to stay cool and get used to it."
"Yeah, of course cool is all good," Heiner said. "But I can't haul myself up and down the stairs each time I'm looking for something. We need to discuss this at the next meeting. "Where the hell is the freakin' drill?"
Heiner muttered something to himself, then he took off again.

Hucky grabbed his guitar and played the intro to "Crying is not Worth It." Every good band needed at least one ballad, that is, a song to breathe, where the fans would wave their lighters. "Crying is not Worth It" was such a ballad, but he didn't have a reasonable solo, yet.
He played the working version of the song on his tape recorder and fast forwarded to the chorus: "... crying ...hy-hy…, is not-worth-it, not-worth-it, not-worth-it …, crying … hy-hy …, is not-worth-it, not-worth-it, not-worth it ..."

Hucky closed his eyes and felt the pain.

He let his fingers wander over the D-minor improvisation scale and occasionally hit the tremolo. Not bad. He wasn't quite there, yet, but was getting closer. Maybe he should try it an octave higher, maybe that would do the trick. Hucky reeled back the tape and let it run again: "... crying ...hy-hy…, is not-worth-it, not-worth-it, not-worth-it …"

Suddenly he remembered where the drill could be. He had seen Kugelblitz using it in the attic. He would pick it up for Heiner. Why make it unnecessarily difficult for him? Hucky went up to the attic and found the drill next to a broken wooden chest.

Heiner was not in his room. He had covered the walls with spiraling, multi-colored triangles that glittered with gold dust - an effect almost like a kaleidoscope. If you looked at it for a while you got dizzy.

On the desk stood a model of a tenement building. Heiner had built the outline of the building with wires. In the center he had placed a cardboard box, representing an elevator.

Hucky heard footsteps. He put the drill on Heiner's bed and left the room. In the corridor he met Kugelblitz.

"His room is kind of crazy, ain't it?"

"Yeah," said Hucky. "Kind of."

Kugelblitz grinned. "In there you can get high without a single drag from Kerm's bong."

Hucky wanted to know what exactly Heiner's problem was. Why did he always walk in a wobble and rowed with his arms. Wasn't there anything that could be done about it? They looked it up in the healthcare dictionary.

Hucky read aloud: "The term spasticity is derived from the Greek word 'Spasmos' (spasm) and describes an increased residual stress in skeletal muscles, which is always due to an injury to the brain."

"Well, I already knew that he had a loose wire up there," Kugelblitz said. "No need to check the dictionary for this."

The article was long and complicated. There were several different spastic types. There were those where only the legs were affected as with Heiner. In others, the arm muscles and sometimes even the muscles of speech were affected as well. There were numerous causes: lack of oxygen at birth, cerebral infarction, accidents with traumatic brain injury. There was only one common denominator - it was incurable.

As Hucky passed the fourth floor, he heard Heiner's voice in Meike's room. Meike sat on her bed with her back against the wall and her legs drawn up. Heiner sat in a chair and leafed through a vegetarian cookbook: "Cream of carrot soup and red beets as a dessert pudding. That sounds delicious."
"True," Meike said. "But I haven't tried it yet."
"Maybe we can do some cooking together sometime, okay?"
"Sure, why not."
Hucky cleared his throat. "Just wanted to say that I found the drill."
Heiner looked up. "Oh, really?"
"It was in the attic."
"That's incredibly nice of you," Heiner said, "it is just of no use for me, now."
"You don't need it anymore?"
"Meike has convinced me that I better use nails."
Heiner turned a page in the cookbook. "Nasi Goreng with tofu steaks, that sounds good."

Hucky left. He looked out the hallway window. Behind the S-Bahn premises lay the cemetery. A few scraps of a funeral march spilled across.

Heiner was a jerk.

27.
THE WATER CONNECTION

As Hucky came into in the kitchen, Heiner was sitting at the table reading a newspaper. Beside him a large bag of bread rolls, butter, jam, and a steaming cup of coffee. Hucky noticed the new faucet over the sink and turned it on.

Water!

Heiner put down the newspaper and grinned. "The waterworks unit was here this morning, but you guys were still asleep."

Pflaume came in, wearing only some baggy briefs and an undershirt.

He stared at the water jet. "Holy cow!" He looked at Heiner. "Did you ...?"

Pflaume stuck his index finger in the jet, as if he wanted to see if it was real. "Not bad, Heiner, not bad."

Pflaume went to the tape recorder and turned it full blast: "London Calling." He walked out of the kitchen and left the door open.

Heiner scrambled to his feet, turned the tape recorder down and closed the door. As he sat down, the door swung open again. Kermit and Kugelblitz came in, Candy, Meike, and Carla. The water story had gone around fast. All stared at the jet coming out of the faucet. It was like Christmas. Perhaps Heiner wasn't so bad after all.

Kermit looked into the big bag full of bread rolls and grabbed some jam and butter. Candy went to the tape recorder and blared it all the way up again.

Pflaume came back, now dressed. He parted the spreads. "Any cold cuts?"

"Take a look in the fridge," Kugelblitz said. "There should be some left."

Pflaume pulled a plate with cold cuts out of the fridge. "Not really my favorite, but whatever."

He dropped a slice of sausage into his mouth.

Heiner took a sip of coffee and looked around. "So, how shall we handle it? Today I've bought breakfast. Who's buying tomorrow?"

All were silent at once. The tape recorder still played "London Calling": "... the ice age is coming, the sun's zooming in ..., engines stop running, the wheat's growing thin ..."

"Somehow we have to make a plan," Heiner said. "I would suggest we set a schedule, so that we buy in turns at a given time."
Candy put her bread roll down. "Listen, sweetie, I buy when it suits me, okay?"
"Yeah, right," Heiner said. "When does it suit you, for example? Then I'll put you down for that day."
"Are you deaf, man," Candy said. "I said, I buy when it suits me, okay?"

Heiner raised his eyebrows. "Oh."

"We always do it like this," Meike said. "Who has money, simply buys something. It's quite easy."
"Yeah, but as a result the fridge will probably be almost always empty" Heiner said. "Just like today."
"So far it has always worked out," Candy said. "Get it?"

Hucky backed away from the discussion. Everyone had to figure it out for themselves. Of course he would never put a chocolate pudding in the fridge, because it was surely gone after half an hour. Therefore he had a secret stash in his room. And everyone else had one, too.

28.
KALLE AND SOCKE

Kalle and Socke showed up on a market day.

Hucky looked out the window. The guy with the bananas shouted: "Come to me, come to me, bananas, nice and big, just two marks. Just two marks the bunch!"

Kalle sat in a wheelchair and Socke maneuvered him through the market. Kalle was fat and had chubby cheeks. He wore a flat cap, and on his ear dangled a small silver skull. Socke was skinny. His thin hair stood out to all sides, and the frame of his horn-rimmed glasses was patched with duct tape. He wore a kilt over his greasy jeans.

Kalle looked up and waved at Hucky. "Can you come down? Need to talk with you guys."
Hucky walked down the stairs. When he reached the ground floor, Heiner was already at the door.
"Welfare told us to come here," said Kalle. "We're supposed to move in."
"Who exactly sent you?" asked Heiner.
Kalle took a letter out of his pocket and handed it over.
Heiner read the letter. He frowned and shook his head.

The Turk from the vegetable stand shouted: "Three kilos for five! Three kilos for five! Yes, young lady, tomatoes, so red, so beautiful, so super tasty!"

Meike and Candy came walking along the street. They had run some errands.

Candy touched Kalle on the shoulder. "Hey, man, don't we know each other?"

"Sure, girl," said Kalle. "We met at the *Bunker*."

"So you're moving in? That would be, like, totally cool."

"Welfare sent us. When I move in, they'll probably even give me more dough."

Meike looked at Socke. "You're moving in, too?"

He nodded. "I'm part of the package."

"Three kilos for five! Three kilos for five!" The Turk shouted again. "Yes, young lady, tomatoes, so red, so beautiful, so super tasty!"

Heiner shook his head. "Very strange that they are already sending someone. We're not even done with the elevator and all."

"Beats me," Kalle said. "With Socke I'll get anywhere."

Heiner folded the letter and shook his head. "Anyway, it's weird."

"Let's go in," Meike said.

Socke took Kalle piggyback, Hucky folded up the wheelchair, and they went up the stairs into the store.

Shortly afterwards, the others arrived as well. They sat on the edge of the stage and on the side benches. No one had anything against Kalle and Socke, some even knew them. They often hung out at Kottbusser Tor and asked for change.

Kalle was a cheerful guy. He constantly laughed and

slapped on the armrests of his wheelchair, which made the silver skull wobble on his ear. Socke was the silent type. Occasionally he scratched his head and grinned.

Heiner sat in the darkest corner of the store, looking annoyed. He cast a longing glance at Meike, who stood next to Kalle and had put her hand on his shoulder.

It seemed like, Heiner was jealous.

29.
THE SHOPPING COMMITTEE

The supermarket was huge, the granite floor freshly waxed. Soft music filled the air, occasionally interrupted by the announcement of a special offer.

Exactly three years ago Falk, Pflaume, and Candy had invaded the abandoned house and started the squat. This had to be celebrated of course. Fortunately they had made a profit with the concert.

On their third anniversary they wanted to do it in style: French Camembert, Chianti Classico, Parma ham, Danish butter, Spanish extra virgin olive oil, and a big fat Polish duck. Their two carts slowly filled up. They had to make sure to not exceed their budget, and Meike wrote the prices for each item on a note pad.

The shopping committee consisted of Meike, Pflaume, Candy, and Hucky. He had only joined, so he could be close to Meike. He missed her. How could he have fallen for a fake like Lilli?

After one hour their two shopping carts were full to the brim.

"Brilliant," Candy said. "Now all we need is the duck, and then we're done."

"We should take more wine perhaps," Pflaume said. "Maybe it's not enough."

"Nonsense," Meike said. "We've got enough."

"Red wine never goes bad," Pflaume said. "Hold on a second. I'd better be on the safe side."

Pflaume ran back to the shelf with the wine. They had long run out of the wine from Candy's sister, but through that free supply they had acquired a taste for it. Red wine also went along well with the duck, of course.

Hucky thought of the family celebrations in Bad Wildungen. Duck was always part of the menu, and almost always there had been a fight of some sort. He remembered a special Christmas celebration years ago. Senior teacher von Hachenstein had paid him guitar lessons, but only for classical guitar - Bach, Händel, Schubert. Hucky saw the decorated Christmas tree in front of him, the flashing lights and the tinsel. He smelled the duck and the freshly baked Christmas cookies. And he saw himself sitting on a chair in front of the whole family. He had one foot on a footstool, essential to keep the right posture for classical guitar.

It was quiet. The flashing Christmas lights emitted a soft rhythmic click. The family was almost complete: Senior teacher von Hachenstein, Hucky's mom, his sister Heidi, and his brownnosing younger brother Helge. Along came uncle Kurt, his wife Elfi, and daughter Christine. And of course there was widow Schulz from next door who had been invited out of Christian charity.

Hucky had tried to avoid the audition, but to no avail. Senior teacher von Hachenstein wanted to see for what he had spent good money. Helge had already recited a Christmas poem, Heidi had played the flute, and now it was

Hucky's turn. He had practiced the sonata The Savior Has Come, for an entire month, first with his teacher at the guitar lesson, then at home.

Hucky stared at the sheet music and then had a sudden blackout. The notes drifted before his eyes, his hands failed to work. He had completely forgotten the sonata. He was sweating. "Can I have a glass of water?"
His sister brought a glass of water from the kitchen. Helge giggled as the old poisonous backstabber he was. Hucky undid the button on the collar of his shirt and loosened the polyester tie that he had put on.

He started to play, but missed a beat right at the second bar. He struggled like hell with the sonata. The lame rhythm, boring melody and artificial posture were the exact opposite of what he really was about. If he'd had it his way he would have played "Anarchy in the UK," and not this antiquated bullshit.
He fumbled on anyway, and tried to play the sonata to its end somehow. After five sheer endless minutes with several screw-ups he had finally made it.

All family members applauded, although it was more out of courtesy. The backstabber giggled again. Hucky felt infinitely miserable. It was simply all wrong with the classical guitar, the footstool, and the polyester tie. On top of it all he later got into a fistfight with Helge and was grounded for two weeks. At exactly that evening he had started to plan his escape to Berlin.

Candy stood on her tippy toes as she pulled a small box from the top row of the shelf.
"Look here a minute," she said. "They have truffles here,

man. Shall we take 'em?"

"You're nuts," Meike said. "They cost twenty-five marks."

"I've never eaten truffles, girl," Candy said. "Ever."

"The stuff does not even taste well anyway," Meike said.

"Whence thou knowest that?" Candy said. "Have you ever eaten truffles?"

"No. But it's definitely not worth it. Put the can back!"

Candy looked at Hucky.

"Do we take 'em? Speak up!"

Hucky shrugged. He had never eaten truffles, either, and he was curious how they tasted, but twenty-five marks for such a small can was quite expensive.

Pflaume came running with the wine. "Hey, hey, hey, truffles," he shouted. "Always my favorite. Sure we're taking them."

He put the can on the shopping cart.

They went to the freezers. There were frozen chicken, beef steaks, vegetables, cakes, ready meals and finally magnificent Polish ducks. Candy grabbed one and lifted it up. "Let's take this one. It looks really swell, I find."

"Perhaps we should take two," Pflaume said. "One is probably not enough."

"That is true, Milord" Candy said.

She took several ducks from the freezer and put them on the floor next to each other. She searched around until she found two about the same size. It was all about the visuals.

Two associates who set up a stall with sweets had noticed the whole thing. They grinned.

Shortly before they reached the cash registers they passed by a sausage stand, and there hung this wonderful Hungarian salami. Hucky's mouth began to water instantly.

"Hmm, that one looks good."

Meike looked at its price tag and checked the numbers in her book. "Yeah, but we don't have enough anymore," she said. "There's not enough for the salami."

"Hmm, salami, salami, salami," Pflaume said.

"But it won't work out," Meike said. "Unless we return the truffles."

"The truffles stay," Pflaume said. "It will sure work out. This time it will!"

He took the salami from the hook and looked around briefly in all directions. Then he threw the sausage with a swing in the air, pulled his jacket forward, said "Plop!" and let the salami fall inside.

30.
THE ANNIVERSARY CELEBRATION

The large table on the stage was set up festively. A white bedding sheet acted as a tablecloth, candles emitted soft light, and incense exuded cinnamon flavor. They had mounted improvised candelabra on the walls, so that the scene looked almost like a medieval banquet.

Hucky was proud of his outfit. He wore a silver cowboy tie over a black shirt and a massive belt with a large silver buckle. He had groomed his hair just like that of young Elvis and, in addition, sported dark sunglasses.

Candy went as Marilyn Monroe. Platinum blonde wig, white summer dress, and beauty mark over her bright red lips. Her cleavage was impressive and you could almost have called her a beauty, were it not for her bad teeth. In celebration of their special day, everyone had to represent an icon of history. Their third anniversary was not just any day, but a beacon of freedom and perseverance, and as such demanded the proper look.

Kugelblitz wore a beret and a khaki military shirt. He had a craggy beard already anyway, and it was not hard to see that this was Che Guevara, twenty pounds overweight.

Kalle and Socke wore bowler hats and suits and went as

Laurel and Hardy. Their outfit was absolutely true to style, but they just couldn't part with two small details: At Kalle's ear still dangled the silver skull and Socke had pulled his kilt over the suit pants.

Carla installed torches at the corners of the stage. She wore a red uniform and a hat with a feather and had painted on a mustache. She looked almost exactly like George Harrison on the Sergeant Pepper cover.

Hucky poured himself some bourbon and smoked a cigar. He would naturally drink red wine with the duck, but as an aperitif bourbon was simply unbeatable. Although the King of Rock 'n Roll was known not to drink alcohol, Hucky still thought that the bourbon went well with his Elvis outfit. He looked into the mirror. Through his dark sunglasses he could hardly see anything, but the glasses were simply a must.

Heiner went as Lawrence of Arabia, which made a lot of sense, since the Arab robe hid his legs. And strangely enough he did not look half bad as a sheik.
Meike represented Cleopatra. She wore a white tunic and a golden crown in form of a snake and had surrounded her eyes with black eyeliner.

Suddenly the door burst open. Kermit and Pflaume came in with the two ducks on sheet trays. It smelled of crispy duck skin and apple filling.
Kermit wore a knitted Jamaican cap, and on his t-shirt sparkled a golden cannabis leaf: Bob Marley in living colors.
Pflaume had laid his Mohawk flat, and combed it to the right. Over his upper lip, he had painted a square little

mustache, and on his baggy undershirt stood in Gothic letters: Adolf.

Frida K. came in. She had recovered by now and went quite classic as, well, Frida Kahlo. She resembled her anyway, but had dressed up just like her in the famous picture with the monkey and the cat.

The only ones still missing were Falk and Lilli.
"Where the hell are they?" Adolf said. "The ducks will get cold, dammit."
He rang their emergency bell, which could be heard in the entire house. "If they don't show up in a minute, we'll start without them."
Suddenly the door opened, squeaking. This corner of the store was very dark and the figure entering could hardly be discerned at first, but then the person slowly stepped into the light. A murmur went through the room.

JESUS CHRIST!

Falk looked exactly like the Savior in church pictures. He raised his hand: "Hallelujah!"

Behind him, another figure slowly appeared with a long, white dress, a white cloth over her hair, her head humbly lowered: Lilli as Virgin Mary.

They sat around the table. The candles flickered and cast a soft light on the illustrious guests.
"The photo!" Bob Marley exclaimed. "Before we begin, we need to take a picture!"
He positioned his old Polaroid camera on their folding ladder, programmed the self-timer and hurried back to the

others. The flash went off, and the camera spit out the photo. Gradually, the image developed on the Polaroid paper. A shiver ran down Hucky's spine. The image corresponded almost exactly to the representation of the Last Supper: Jesus was positioned in the center, and around him sat the disciples. Hucky counted the people present: Jesus plus twelve. The twelve disciples. Was this a coincidence?

Jesus stood up and tapped a fork against his glass. Slowly the room went quiet.
"Cheers to the house!" Jesus exclaimed.
"Cheers to the house!" They toasted and drank.
Jesus raised his glass again. "Cheers to T.T. Embargo!"
"Cheers to T.T. Embargo!" echoed the answer.
"And above all, cheers to ..." Falk made a dramatic pause and raised his arms. Everyone looked at him intently. He savored the moment to the last, the tension was almost unbearable.
"Above all, cheers to what ...?" Che Guevara said impatiently. "To what, spit it out, man!" Kugelblitz had started drinking while cooking and was already slightly drunk.

"To LOVE, of course!" Falk exclaimed. "Cheers to LOVE!" He grabbed the Virgin Mary and kissed her passionately.

Suddenly the scene developed into some sort of a kissing orgy. Adolf kissed Marilyn, Che Guevara kissed Frida Kahlo, and Bob Marley kissed George Harrison.
Hucky looked at Meike. This time she did not avoid his gaze. The torches reflected in her black-rimmed Cleopatra eyes. Hucky took off his sunglasses and wanted to say

something, but Meike shut his mouth.

"Not now, Holger."

Hucky froze. He absolutely never mentioned his real name, Bad Wildungen, or his family. He was simply Hucky of T.T. Embargo, and that's that. How did Meike know his name?
They looked at each other silently. Meike pulled her hand from his mouth and kissed him passionately. A wonderful feeling. Almost like his first kiss ever.

Shortly after, the party developed into a kind of peck festival, similar to what must have gone on at the court of Louis XIV. Marilyn gave Laurel and Hardy a peck, the Virgin Mary embraced Bob Marley, and Frida Kahlo kissed Jesus. Everyone gradually kissed everyone, and Kugelblitz and Hucky fell into their arms and held each other tight.
"I always wanted to tell you, that ..." Che Guevara fought back tears.
Elvis swallowed and said: "Sure, man ... I know!"
They hugged a little harder still and slapped each other on the shoulder.

Only Lawrence of Arabia sat isolated in his chair. No one hugged him, no one gave him a peck. He sipped his wine and stared down at the table.
Meike went up to him and gave him a peck. "Thanks for the water connection," she said. "And thanks for the contract."
She pulled Heiner off his chair. "Cheers to Heiner," she exclaimed. "Without whom we probably would not be here today!"
Heiner was a bit wobbly on his feet and held out his glass

of red wine in the middle of the table. It was suddenly quiet. Nothing moved, only the wine in his glass slightly trembled. Lawrence of Arabia looked around, searching for eye contact. What if no one would toast with him?

A bus drove past the house. The stage trembled slightly.

Falk put a hand on Heiner's shoulder. "Thank you, brother. I have to admit that we have underestimated you. Cheers!" He knocked glasses with Heiner, and everybody else did as well, even Candy and Pflaume.
Heiner emptied his glass in one gulp and sat down again. Tears rolled down his cheeks.

At dinner they spoke only the bare essentials. It was like a silent agreement, no one broke it. They just enjoyed the culinary delicacies.
Che Guevara gnawed on a drumstick, his hands and his mouth were greasy.
Adolf shoveled apple filling in his mouth, munched a few times and took a sip of wine.
Marilyn feasted on tagliatelle with truffle slices. She had found the recipe in a cookbook. The truffles were finely cut with a razor blade so that you could almost see through them.
"Awesome," Marilyn munched. "I could get used to this, folks." Suddenly one of the tagliatelle fell from the fork into her cleavage. She wanted to fish it out, but Adolf did not let her. He buried his head in her cleavage and sucked up the noodle with his thick lips.

Hucky tried a bit of everything: duck, truffle pasta, egg salad with mustard sauce and occasionally a slice of salami. It was all exquisite. On this day everything was just right.

141

Che Guevara stood up and raised his arms. "Now lights out, and everybody close your eyes!"
Jesus looked at him, puzzled. "Lights out? Why?"
Che Guevara jumped off the stage and walked toward the wardrobe. "Lights out and eyes closed. Otherwise it will not work."
They extinguished all candles and torches. It was now pitch dark.
"Do not look," Kugelblitz exclaimed. "You can only look after I say so!"
Hucky heard Kugelblitz coming up the creaky wooden steps. "Okay, ready, steady, go!"
They opened their eyes. In the middle of the table stood a magnificent cream pie.

On top three burning candles and the anarchist "circle A".

A general "Ooohhhhh" went through the ranks.
"Brilliant," Marilyn exclaimed. "Simply brilliant!"

Che Guevara stood up and composed himself. He was almost completely wasted by now, but he wanted to say something. He suddenly had a hiccup. Anyway, he began to speak:
"The mighty and the powerful of this world, hic ..."
He paused for a moment and looked around.
"They can tear out one little rose ... hic, they can, hic, tear out two little roses, hic ..."
He cleared his throat. "Fucking hiccups, man."
He looked around. His gaze was suddenly empty. "Uh, screw it," he said, and sat down. "Bon apetit!"

Finally, they played the tape with Kermit's "Party Mix for the After Hours." Most of the candles had already burned down, and only one torch was still lit.

And then, miraculously, another bottle of vodka appeared. Everything fit together perfectly that evening, and when "I Am Sailing" came up, passion came into play. Rod Steward was always a surefire recipe. "I am sailing stormy waters ... ... to be near you, to be free ..."

Adolf danced with Marilyn, cuddling and massaging her buttocks. Jesus made out with the Virgin Mary, French kissing her while dancing. Che Guevara gyrated with Frida K. over the floor and nuzzled his cheek gently against hers.

Bob Marley danced with George Harrison, and Elvis with Cleopatra. Even Laurel and Hardy were dancing. Kalle illustrated the song with his arms, and Socke rhythmically moved the wheelchair around.

Lawrence of Arabia was spinning in a circle with his flowing Arab robe, smoking a joint and singing loudly: "I am flying ... I am flying ... like a bird 'cross the sky ..."

Elvis was drunk.

Hucky had guzzled half a bottle of bourbon, emptied countless glasses of red wine, and then he topped it all off with several shots of vodka. He suddenly buckled, and had Cleopatra not supported him, he would have fallen. Damn dancing. The movement had brought the potent mixture in his stomach into action.

Lawrence of Arabia was also totally wasted. He flipped the stump of his joint into a corner, threw his arms into the air and sang at the top of his lungs: "Can you hear me ..., can you hear me ..., through the dark night, far away ..."

Elvis felt dreadfully wretched. He broke away from Meike, leaned against the wall and took a breath. Sweat on his forehead. The music and the voices around him faded "... to be near you, to be free ..."

He staggered past Meike, stumbled through the door into the yard and almost stepped on a chicken, which jumped off, cackling.

He leaned his head against a tree and pulled the cowboy tie from his neck. And then it all came out, the duck, the truffle pasta, the egg salad, the salami, the cream pie, and all the other stuff. It all gushed out, and he could hardly breathe. Hucky choked and spat, choked and spat, until he didn't have a single morsel of the feast in his belly. He somehow dragged himself into his room and fell into his bed, semi-unconscious.

He would not sleep long.

31.
THE ABYSS

The siren was terribly loud. Hucky came up and touched his head, the pain was almost unbearable.

The siren kept on howling. What the heck was going on? He opened the window and looked down: an ambulance from the fire department.

Hucky stumbled down the stairs. The others were standing on the third floor. He slid between Pflaume and Kermit, and then he saw it: Heiner lay motionless on the second floor stairway. He was still wearing the Arab robe, only his headgear had fallen off. His limbs were twisted, his face bloodied, but he was still breathing. A feather in front of his mouth moved slightly back and forth. The cats sometimes tore pigeons, leaving scattered feathers in the aisles.

The firefighters put Heiner onto a stretcher. He looked up and moved his lips, as if he wanted to say something, but nothing came out.
Kugelblitz pointed to a broken part in the handrail. "Somehow he must have fallen down from there."
The wood of the handrail had been rotten for some time already but they didn't have money for repairs.

Hucky noticed that Meike was missing. He suspected that

she had something to do with Heiner's plunge and went to her room. She lay in bed, face buried in hands. "It wasn't my fault, he damn scared me to death."

She sat up and stared out the window. "You were suddenly gone, right, and then ... I danced with him, and I thought, how does he do this with his legs, ... I mean dancing, but then I was tired, suddenly I'm so tired, and I go, go up to my room. I lie in bed, right, I sleep, right, and then ... He is suddenly on top of me. I wake up and see his eyes, right above me. He is on top of me, directly on top of me, and I, I push him away, push him out, out, out, push him into the hall, push him away ... out, out, out ..., and it..., he stumbles, right, he falls, right, falls against the handrail and ..."

Meike looked at Hucky. "He damn scared me to death, his eyes ..."

32.

AS LUCK WOULD HAVE IT

Three weeks later, Hucky, Pflaume, and Kugelblitz peered through a crack in the construction fence. There was a deep pit where their house had once stood. Everything was gone, even the trees in the yard.

Kugelblitz spat on the floor, and Pflaume flicked his cigarette butt into the vacant lot. They were on their way to the rehearsal room and carried their instruments. It was cloudy and muggy. It had rained during the night.

"Wait a minute," Pflaume said. "What's this?" He pushed his drumstick through a crack in the fence and pointed to a small round thing. It was smack in the middle of the pit.

Kugelblitz and Pflaume pulled the boards of the fence apart, and Hucky squeezed through the gap. He trotted down the slope, and grabbed the tuning knob of his old tube radio. The knob was made of Bakelite, golden in the middle, black on the side. The radio had been working properly, still, and the speakers had been excellent. but the cops had had no use for it. He put the knob in his pocket and scrambled back up the embankment.

Ismail and Tarik came out of the Karadeniz and crossed the street. Although only three weeks had passed since the eviction, it felt as if they had not seen each other for ages.

148

Hucky still owed Ismail almost sixty marks, but he did not have them at the moment. The Turk didn't mind: "Can you bring by later, brother."

A black station wagon stood parked across the street. Two men put a large black bag on a stretcher. Gerlinde Steinmöller had passed away a few days after the eviction. The neighbors had only recently noticed the odor and the flies on the window pane.

As the hearse drove off, Hucky spontaneously raised his hand in a last farewell. The others seemed to understand the gesture and did the same. Sure, the old hag had made their lives miserable, but in the face of death, composure and respect had to prevail.
The hearse drove through a puddle, and the dirty water splashed up to the group in a high arc. All five jumped to the side, but everyone got splattered. Tarik's favorite jersey from *Izmirspor* had been stained, and he cursed in Turkish.

Gerlinde Steinmöller had done it again - one last time.

Suddenly a summer rain poured down and it started to thunder. They could not possibly walk to the rehearsal room in this torrential rain and quickly ran over to the Karadeniz. They drank tea and nibbled on some Turkish baklava.

For a while they had considered starting a new squat and had searched half the city, but there were simply no more vacant buildings, and the remaining squats were all full to the brim.

Kalle and Socke had not wanted to stay in a home for the

handicapped, and preferred to sleep in the park. All others temporarily stayed at the weekend garden shack of Carla's uncle. They slept in tents on the lawn. The shack was in Lichtenrade in the middle of nowhere, but it had at least S-Bahn connection.

Heiner had recovered after a week. He had gotten off lightly - a broken arm, two knocked out teeth. Once they had seen him in front of Tommy Weissbecker Haus. Pflaume totally freaked out and wanted to beat him up, but the others had held him back.

The torrential rain was finally over. Hucky, Pflaume, and Kugelblitz said good bye to the Turks and grabbed their instruments.

At the youth center rehearsal room, there were amps and drums. You could use the space for free, but had to sign up in advance in a calendar.
Falk was not there, yet. Occasionally he and Lilli stayed with his brother in Zehlendorf, and he almost always came late.

Hucky played the intro to "Sometimes Cold, Sometimes Hot." Kugelblitz fell in with his bass and Pflaume with the drums. "Living in a squat, dududu-duuh, dududu-duuh... sometimes cold, sometimes hot, dududu-duuh, dududu-duuh..."
It was strange, but now that they had no house, the song sounded kind of weak. Then came the solo. Hucky closed his eyes and cranked up the volume. After a few seconds he hit a wrong note and broke off. They started again from the beginning. "Living in a squat, dududu-duuh, dududu-duuh..., sometimes cold, sometimes hot, dududu-duuh,

dududu-duuh ..."
Suddenly, one of the volunteers from the youth center stood in the doorway. "Phone call for T.T. Embargo. Make it short, please."
Kugelblitz grabbed the handset. The extension cord of the phone barely reached into the rehearsal room.

It was Falk.

Forty-five minutes later they were in Dahlem, a hidden side street. They forced their way through the hole in the fence - just like Falk had described it - and marched through thick brush to the back entrance of the abandoned mansion.
The house obviously had been vacant for years. The roof was broken in places, and it rained through.

Some rooms were overgrown with plants. The fixtures in the bathroom and kitchen had been dismantled, and a few rusty wires hung from the ceiling.

Lilli sat on an upturned crate as she rolled a joint, and Falk threw a burning piece of paper into the old fireplace.

The flue worked.

Lilli passed on the joint, and Falk inhaled holding in the smoke. "The shack's a bit weathered," he said, coughing. "But we could fix it up a bit, couldn't we?"

ABOUT THE AUTHOR

In the 1980s Matthias Drawe lived in a squatted house in West Berlin. From 1995 to 2010 he was based in New York City and reported from around the world for Deutschland Radio Berlin (German NPR).

The scope of his work includes human interest stories, travel reports, and screenplays for tv and film.

Currently he lives in Rio de Janeiro.

BERLIN IN THE 1980s

By Charles M. Miller

I lived in West Berlin as an American ex-pat in the 80s. At the time it was one of the strangest places on earth.

The division of the city was a result of the division of Germany after the Second World War. Even though it was the Soviet Red Army that conquered Berlin, the Western Allies had made it clear that they wanted half of it. The Eastern part became the Soviet sector, and the Western part was divided into the American, British, and French sectors.

West Berlin had a special status from the outset. It was de facto associated with West Germany though governed by the Four Power Agreement. Residents of West Berlin could not be drafted into the West German military and they could not vote in West German elections.

In the fifties it became clear that the West was on the winning side when it pulled off an "economic miracle" which was fueled by American money (Marshall Plan). The East was dirt poor in comparison, in part because the Soviets had dismantled most of the factories as reparations. As a consequence, many people voted with their feet and fled to the West.

The border between East and West Germany was easy to control since it went through rural areas but the "leak" in Berlin seemed impossible to plug. Public transportation went from one part of the city to the other and the border went right through densely populated inner city areas, sometimes cutting streets or even houses in half. Each month thousands of people fled to West Berlin and East Germany was about to collapse.

In the early morning of August 13, 1961, with the backing of the Soviets, the East German government started building a fence around West Berlin, thereby closing it off.

The Americans immediately rolled up with tanks at the checkpoints only to be greeted by Soviet tanks on the other side. Nobody wanted to start a new war, thus the building of the Wall went ahead.

At the beginning, there were frantic attempts from East Germans to still escape to the West resulting in several deaths. As time went by, the East Germans perfected the Wall and made it almost impossible to cross. They tore down everything close to the Wall on the Eastern side and established a "death strip" with land mines and booby-traps. Border guards had orders to shoot in case of an attempt to escape. The drastic measure of building the Wall eventually helped to stabilize East Germany.

When I arrived in West Berlin the Wall had been in place for more than 20 years. I was a young American from the heartland (Kentucky, to be precise) and instead of going to New York or Paris I decided to go to West Berlin. By then, the news had spread that it was a weird place and I was very curious.

It was even weirder than expected. I settled in Kreuzberg, close to the Wall, and it seemed like not much had changed there since the end of the war. Most of the buildings were pre-war and almost all of them still had bullet marks. Often, there were huge wooden entrance doors with a special kind of key. It had not one, but two bits, one on each side. You would open the door with the first bit, push the key through the hole to the other side and then close with the bit on the opposing end. Only if you locked the door on the inside could you pull out the key again: security before the age of the intercom.

Once you were in, there were some stairs going up for the front building. That's where you found the good, spacious apartments with lots of light and a view to the street. Walking further you would get to a backyard with other stairs leading up the backyard buildings. In some cases there was even a second backyard or a third one. If you lived on one of the lower stories of those buildings, you would hardly ever see the sun.

Needless to say that I ended up in one of the backyard buildings, first, like most of the newcomers. It was a small studio with the toilet outside half a flight down. It was shared with the residents of the adjacent apartment. There was no hot water and no shower, just a sink. You were supposed to wash up with a cloth or to go to a public bath. For heat, there was a behemoth of a tile stove, which you would fire up with coal briquettes. In many ways it was still like before World War I. In other words: I loved it.

It was certainly a totally different world than what I had known in the U.S. What immediately struck me were the bakeries. At practically every corner you would find one, and they had a huge variety of bread and rolls, at least twenty different kinds. And man, was this bread delicious. Especially for somebody who had only tasted "Wonderbread" up to that point.

And then there was the beer of course. Too many varieties to name them all, and often it was cheaper than water! In a local bar a small draft beer would set you back 90 pfennigs, a mineral water one mark.

In stark contrast to the old substance of the buildings stood the young and colorful scene on the street: independent art

157

galleries, trendy cafes and bars, live venues for all kinds of music, health food stores, bike repair shops. The subway station "Kottbusser Tor" was a meeting point for hardcore punks and junkies, and in between that mix were scores and scores of Turks, both young and old. In Kreuzberg you did not need any German, you could survive entirely on Turkish. There were Turkish merchants for everything, even Turkish banks, pharmacies, and doctors.

West Berlin was much larger than I had expected. It could easily take two hours by public transportation to get from one end of the Wall to the other. The city was so huge that it even had its own forest, where you could run into wild hogs and deer. And it had a lake so big that it was hard to make out the other side.

In order to get to the outskirts of the city you would take the S-Bahn (short for "Stadt-Bahn" or "City Train"). The wagons were bigger than those of the subway, and the train rode above ground, only in the dense inner-city areas would it dive underground. As part of the old railway system it was run by East Germany who had inherited the former "Deutsche Reichsbahn" (German Imperial Railway). They made a loss running the S-Bahn in West Berlin but kept it anyway to maintain their claim on Berlin in its entirety.

Taking an S-Bahn trip would send you decades back. The trains were almost exactly like they had been in pre-war times, they had wooden benches and tubular iron radiators which made odd cracking sounds. The tickets were printed on greyish East German cardboard, a type of paper you could not find in the West try as you might. Needless to say that I loved the S-Bahn.

The public transportation system in West Berlin was weirder than anyone could imagine. In order to get from the North of West Berlin to its South, you would have to travel under the midtown section of East Berlin since this is where the pre-war tracks for the lines were located. Both, the subway and the S-Bahn dove under the mid-section of East Berlin, passed closed-off "ghost stations" guarded by machine gun-wielding East German soldiers, only to dive back up in West Berlin.

But it got even weirder than that. At one of the underground stations, Friedrichstrasse, you could actually get off the train. You could switch lines there and you could buy heavily discounted Western liquor and cigarettes at an East German run "Intershop." It had been established in order to obtain desperately needed hard currency. The store was extremely popular with West Berlin punks and people with limited means who bought their supply of booze and smokes there.

On the upstairs floor of Friedrichstrasse there was a border checkpoint into East Berlin. Westerners were allowed to cross if they complied with the 1:1 exchange rate of 25 East marks for 25 West marks (the black market rate was 5:1). For this "entrance fee," as the West Berliners called it, you could stay for 24 hours in East Berlin. East Germans on the other hand were not allowed to cross into West Berlin unless they had a special permission, which was only granted in extremely rare cases.

Out of curiosity I went to East Berlin but it was not really a very cheerful place. You had the feeling that you passed into an entirely different world. It was grey, ugly and

159

uniform. People were generally dressed in drab clothes, and the low-tech East German cars left an unpleasant smell in the air. Restaurants only served very basic fare and you often had to wait in long lines to get a table. The bad mood of East German wait staff was legendary. In the shops there was not much to buy. They actually did have some items in the window but when you went in to actually purchase something, they were out of stock.

It was all a big lie. The state run media proclaimed the East a socialist paradise on a winning streak and presented the West as a rotten capitalist snake pit on the verge of collapse. East Berlin had not much to offer to me and after two visits I never went back.

West Berlin on the other hand was capitalism at its best, at least in the area around Kurfürstendamm (West Berlin's luxury shopping street). There you could find whatever your heart desired. It was no problem to party the entire night and burn the candle on both ends - and in the middle. Thanks to the Americans who wanted it to be a "Window of the West" it was the only German city without a curfew.

West Berlin's boroughs had quite different flavors. In Wilmersdorf you would find mostly old people, many of them war-time widows. The shops and cafes in that area showed it: everything was staunchly conservative. In Charlottenburg and Schöneberg you would find established artists, state sponsored theaters and museums, the opera house and the Berlin Philharmonics. Wedding and Neukölln were populous working class districts with lots of Turkish immigrants but void of an alternative scene.

My turf was Kreuzberg. It was full of aspiring artists from all around the globe and even Iggy Pop and David Bowie lived there for a while. Kreuzberg was also home to the majority of squat houses and it was easy to see that the forefront of the avant garde lived there, the coolest of the cool. Why pay rent when you could as well invade a vacant building and make it your own?

Shortly after the construction of the Wall, West Berlin had steadily lost inhabitants, mainly middle class families who found it inconvenient and frightening to live in a closed-in city. This void was quickly filled by draft dodgers, all kinds of artists who were drawn by the special status of the city, and foreign workers, mostly Turks.

The great majority of the vacant buildings in West Berlin had been bought by speculators who preferred to keep them unoccupied and make a killing when East Germany would collapse one day, and Berlin as a whole would become the capital of the unified Germany again. At the same time there was a shortage of affordable housing. Because of that situation many found it morally justified to invade those buildings, even though it was technically illegal.

Charles M. Miller
New York City, September 2014

Made in the USA
Charleston, SC
25 May 2015